The Adventure Now Begins. . . .

Ishaan
Sahai

Star Voyagers
Book One

The Voyagers Unite

By Author of *Space Explorers*:
Ishaan Sahai

Star Voyagers:
The Voyagers Unite

Dedicated to future astronauts, astronomers and authors of the world as well as my parents, who inspired me and led me all the way.

-I.S.

Super Computer Accessing Database...100% Loaded:
Contents

Chapter 1
Training

2001 AD- At the Kuiper Belt, a gap appeared on the side of an asteroid like a tunnel. An Unknown Flying Object was flying towards this hole. It was a hollow asteroid, and weird organisms were everywhere. They had a brown body with a human-shape. Their heads were horizontal ovals, and they had the same amount of hands and legs as a human.

The "asteroid" had metal roofs, flooring, and walls in the exterior. As the space ship flew through the tunnel, the gap closed behind it. The hollow area grew larger and brighter as the space ship got closer. The space ship was getting slower as well. It approached the floor, leveled itself, extended legs, and touched down. Smoke flew everywhere.

"On the Earth's moon, the filthy humans have landed on the surface in the Earth Year 1969 AD," said the co-leader. He was the one who had just walked out the UFO. The co-leader had the same shape as any other of the creatures. He had a deep voice. When all the surrounding smoke cleared, you could see that the UFO was a long, grey, mechanical oval and had a glass dome at the top center. Peering inside, you would notice that it was very technologically advanced. "It has taken me over 50 Earth Years to get here with this information. Soon they'll find out about the water on the moon if exploration continues. It may happen in the Earth

Year 2009 AD. However, I think we shall attack one decade from now- in the Earth Year 2011 AD."

So, they began preparing for the conflict.

*****

January 31st 2010 AD- Michael smiled. He had tidy black hair. Right in front of him was the Astronomical Voyagers Academy. There, participants will train themselves to face space and five lucky people will own a unique *Star Speeder* that can handle many extremes that the average spacecraft can't, is more technologically advanced, and (did he mention it's the coolest?). It can't handle all extremes, but it can handle more than any other spacecraft.

Michael wanted to own that *Star Speeder* more than anything else. Michael was really intelligent about Astronomy and knew almost anything you'd want to know related to space. If there was anyone who could own that *Star Speeder*, it was him. He wanted to be an astronaut since he was four, and knew a lot then! He continued inside the building and confirmed his name at a registration office, where he got a map. "Wow," he said. "This place is huge! I think I need to go to the meeting office next to the training room."

So, he walked to the room. While he was, he looked around. Dozens of people were going this way and that. It seemed like a pretty modern building. For the first time, he noticed it was more high-tech than he could ever imagine. Besides the people, there were also robots, which could walk, talk, fly, and, in fact, seemed to be capable of nearly everything!

Finally, he arrived in the meeting room. There were hundreds of chairs. The seats had reserved signs with full names. Michael noticed there were only four people in the whole room yet and all of them were sitting in the front row. Michael finally found his name in the front row. Two people were sitting on each side of him, and they were the ones Michael had originally seen. The first person on his right side was a woman with black hair and a pony tail. The first person on his left side was also a female, but had long brown hair. Next to each of the girls sat two boys. On the left was an Indian with black hair, glasses and curious eyes; on the right was someone with brown hair. Michael saw that they had name tags, and their names were: Anne, with the black hair and ponytail, Jane, with the black hair, Rohit, the Indian and James, with brown hair. Michael wondered where they got the name tags, so he searched for one. Underneath his chair was a name tag with his name on it. So, he put it on and checked his wristwatch. It was 10:00 am. That meant that there was one hour left before they would be given a speech. He thought he'd spend the time getting to know the four people around him. Anyways, there was also nothing else to, since most people wouldn't come for about thirty minutes. They seemed to get along good. At 10:55 he was still getting to know Rohit.

"Really, Ro-hat?" Michael was saying.

"Yeah, but my name isn't Ro-hat, its pronounced Ro-hith."

"Let me see if I'm right. Ro-hit."

"Close. Ro-hith."

"Okay, Ro-hith."

"Good job, Michael!" Rohit said sarcastically.

Finally, the meeting started. A person stood at a podium to begin his speech. It was hard to tell how he looked like, since it was dark in that area of the room. "Hello, hello everyone. Now settle down. QUIET BACK THERE, PLEASE. I'm glad you could all participate in this exclusive event. As you probably know, this only happens once in a decade," The whole room echoed with his booming voice. "And you should also know that you get a one-of-a-kind *Star Speeder*. The details are all in the pamphlet you got. I'll re-explain it so that we're all on the same page. Hundreds of you entered, but only fifty extraordinary out of you will get a chance in your teams of five, and only five of you get the *Star Speeder*. Oh, and also, only one of you can actually, legally 'OWN' it. I wonder which one of you it'll be. Whoever it is, he or she is very lucky. Now, if you all would be kind enough to follow me into the training room...."

So, everyone squeezed through a narrow door into a humongous room. Finally, they stopped next to a MAT. A MAT is a device which you sit in, but then you'll be spun in crazy directions in order to train yourself for the anti-gravity in outer-space. It took more than half an hour for everyone to get a turn, and they all felt a bit dazed at the end. However, they still could walk half way across the room to a large orange submarine with windows and a hatch at the top to enter it. The guy who gave the speech asked them all to come on in. Suddenly, a dome opened from the ceiling above them, and the vessel flew through it to a deep, large pool filled with water.

Inside, the participants put on scuba diving gear to make them feel as if they were in space. Several went outside as if they were doing a space walk. It felt like an actual space mission. Underwater, they also repaired a telescope, pretended to fly (like weightlessness), and powered a jet pack.

The next training phase was the fly-o-matic. It created air which would make you float to the ceiling, like a wind tunnel. There, they used the jet pack again and sort of swam in the air. Then, they went to a dining hall to have lunch, since it was 1:30 pm. In the dining hall, everyone had a fantastic feast, and you could almost call it an "All You Can Eat" buffet.

They resumed training at 2:30. They visited dozens of training styles. Soon, people began whining that it was becoming boring, but Michael found it really fun. He knew that with that attitude, the people who whined would definitely not even get a chance to be short listed into the fifty people who had a chance to get the *Star Speeder*.

The training finally stopped at 9:30 pm. At this point, even people like Michael were getting tired. The participants went into the meeting room, where the person who gave the speech would tell who the lucky fifty were.

"Now, you should know this, but just to make sure, I'll tell you. There are ten teams, each consist of five people. They get several practices in February. Then, on the last day of the month, there's a show off- a contest, pretty much. The participants who don't get to be in a team get to give the teams points, like voting. The team with the most points gets awarded the *Star Speeder*! You may be wondering how I select

9

you, and that's because during your training today, I've been observing several of you. Also, when I call the people in a team, I call it in a certain order. The first person is the captain or owner of the *Star Speeder*. During the training, though, the person would be the boss. The second person would be the co-captain. The third person would be a regular astronaut. The fourth person would be the data collector, who'd find information about a certain thing and works up most of the technical stuff. The fifth person would also be an astronaut. The reason you got these titles is because, if you win, that's the position you'd get. Well, now let's begin. Team One:..."

Michael dreamt what'd happen if he became the captain and won the *Star Speeder*. But he expected that even if he got short listed to a team which could win the *Star Speeder* that he won't be the captain, which was a big dream for him since his early childhood. He didn't expect to be THAT good. The announcing of the teams carried on for a while.

"And Team Ten: Michael, Anne, Jane, Rohit, and James! That's the last of the teams. Oh- and team ten will meet on the first, the fourteenth, the twentieth, and the twenty-sixth."

Michael couldn't believe his own ears. He *was* the captain, and his new friends made up the rest of the team.

"Nice try, other participants," said Jack, who Michael just recalled was the name of the announcer. "Today, you'll have to go home, but you can try again in two thousand twenty. Oh, and teams; you have some nice rooms to stay in."

So, Michael led Anne, Jane, Rohit, and James to a door. Engraved on the wood was the number ten. Michael turned a key which Jack had given him and went inside, flicking on the lights. Their room was the size of ten huge master bedrooms! It had five comfy beds, a large window that'd let you look outside the building, two bathrooms, and a robot helper. The best part, the robot helper would help them feel at home by designing the room their way.

The next day, the team would begin training. But first, they went to the dining room to have a Breakfast Buffet. All the training phases were the same as the other day, except extremely difficult and mission one was completely changed into something very hard. It turned into a mini-version of the *Star Speeder*, and it would actually take you to certain safe locations in space. How exactly does the *Star Speeder* look like? Well, it is like a large, grey oval flat on its side-turned horizontally. Then, it has ten steel bars poking out from the oval. There's two short ones in the center, four medium-sized ones on its sides, and four long ones on the sides of that. More, they're pairs of bars in an arch pattern. Then, there are large football shaped pods connected to the bars, and you could see through it using a window on the front of the pods. The captain sits in the center pod, on his right sits the co-captain, and on her right is the data collector; on the captain's left is the regular astronaut, and the other astronaut. Michael loved having the simulation of the *Star Speeder*, and was amazed by the beauty of space.

The teams were allowed to see other team practices, but couldn't train at that time. Once, Team Ten came to see Team Nine's practice. The captain was named Ronald. There's something odd about his name, however. Ronald was his last name, and his first name was Watson! Since saying Watson Ronald is weird, everyone calls him by his last name. Well, anyways, Michael was impressed. Ronald is also very good, and so is his team. They're just like Michael and his team, except Ronald uses his knowledge in a bad way, so Team Ten decided not to like his team. And, being bad is probably the reason Team Nine always gets second in everything, whereas Team Ten gets first place. So, Michael and Ronald became rivals for the rest of the month.

Before the teams knew it, it was already the last day of February. The rejected participants came back to vote for the teams. Both the participants and the teams were surprised when they discovered that Jack was the only judge. Both Jack and the participants voted on key pads. Then, everyone's votes were combined to create the teams' average.

Have I told you about the fifteen competition phases? You may know about the MAT, Mission, and the fly-o-matic phases, but not the other twelve. I'll tell you now:

Galactic War- In this training phase, special robot alien dummies will try to destroy the mini *Star Speeder*, so you have to try to destroy them first! Your team will get a hundred points worth instead of ten, because this training phase has ten parts, creating ten training phases.

Orbit Clutch Breaker- This also takes place in the *Star Speeder*. The teams' *Star Speeder* gets locked into an orbit. They have to try to break the clutch.

Repairing In Anti-Gravity- The team members have to huddle together. Then, a glass tube surrounds them all the way to the ceiling. Inside the tubes, there wasn't too much gravity. Their objective: repair a telescope.

In the competition, teams one through eight weren't very good, so let's skip to the averages of Teams Nine and Ten's average.

During the MAT phase, team nine got eight, and team ten got ten. Then, in the mission phase, team nine got nine, whereas team ten got nine and a half. Next came the fly-o-matic, which was where team nine got seven and team ten got ten. In the galactic war, team nine got ninety, and team ten got ninety-five. In the orbit clutch breaker phase, team nine got nine and a half, while team ten got ten. And finally, in the repairing in anti-gravity competition phase, team nine got nine and a half, and team ten got ten.

Finally, at 6:00 pm, the competition stopped.

Everyone went inside the meeting room. There, Jack announced the totals. Soon, he got to teams nine and ten. "Team Nine has got a total of: 127.5," Jack said. "And finally, Team Ten has a total of: 144.5. And our winner is: Michael Jefferson's Team Ten! Team Ten, will you please come up onto the stage?"

So, Team Ten came up to the podium. Jack made Michael swear that he'd only use the *Star Speeder* for good, and only good. Then, Jack handed over the keys to Michael, and shook his and the rest of team members' hands-who were now the *Star Speeder* crew. Everyone else clapped for a long time.

13

Michael knew that it wasn't a dream and that he really owned the *Star Speeder*, but what he didn't know was what was going to happen next January.

Chapter 2
New Year's Day

2011 AD- Michael smiled. It was New Years Day, and he was looking out the window at beautiful white snow fall. He remembered that last year, he gained ownership to a unique, one-of-a-kind, *Star Speeder*. Suddenly, his smile faded. Not only had he never flown it, but he hadn't seen Anne, Jane, Rohit, and James since he got the keys. So, he wanted to start off the New Year *special*....

Michael headed towards his telephone and picked up the receiver. Thirty minutes later, all of the gang were inside Michael's really large garage. "You know what I think?" Michael said. 'I think that perhaps I want to start the New Year off special for all of us, and that's why I called you here. I think that we should head on the *Star Speeder* to space. I put the keys in my pocket somewhere; here they are!"

His thumb headed towards the "Open" button, but then hesitated. But everybody insisted to open the *Star Speeder*, so he pressed the button.

Wind was blowing from the top of the *Star Speeder*. A lever was turning part of the top of the oval. Soon, it had turned into a plank where they could walk inside. Michael went first. When he got to the top, he saw a door where the plank had been. In this door, there was a keyhole, so Michael inserted his keys and opened the door. Inside, there was a ladder, so he decided to walk down. The *Star*

Speeder was dark, so Michael felt around until he touched an electricity control panel. It was hard to make out what was inside, but he thought they were wires. All of them were attached to their proper places, but one wire was loose. So, Michael took the wire and inserted it in a socket. Suddenly, light filled the *Star Speeder*. "Whoa!" he said.

Five minutes later, the rest of the crew decided to go inside, so they walked up the plank, though the door, and down the ladder. James was the last one, so he closed the door, which locked by itself.

When they were all nice and settled: their reaction was, "Whoa!"

The inside of the *Star Speeder* was really high tech. They looked around the area, while the plank returned to its spot above the oval. The crew noticed that there were special space suits that fit perfectly inside a closet. Next, they were eager to see their pods. So, they looked underneath their feet and saw some doors, and opened them. Inside, there were two ladders that took place in the bars. The crew climbed down to their pods. Each pod had a big window, a hologram super computer on the window, a seat, and a large control desk that spread out as a large "C". Michael found this way better than those training phases. Soon, the crew agreed that they were ready to head to outer space.

So, Michael pushed forward on a thrust lever, making sure the garage door was open so he could move out before the door closed. First, the *Star Speeder* slowly moved up a few centimetres, but then zoomed past the atmosphere into the darkness of space.

They wanted to go star gazing in stars, so they decided to go past their solar system and see nebulas, galaxies, red giants, white dwarfs, star clusters, black holes, (the *Star Speeder* could actually break the clutch of a couple of black holes, and luckily, they never got sucked into one), and more. The *Star Speeder* was the one and only that could actually go way faster than the speed of light.

So, Michael pushed another lever to make the *Star Speeder* move at top-speed. The *Star Speeder* vibrated, and went past the Moon, Mars, the Asteroid Belt, Jupiter, Saturn, Uranus, Neptune, Dwarf Planets, Comets, and the Kuiper belt. They were going so fast that they didn't notice Unidentified Flying Objects headed towards Earth.

Everyday, the crew visited different galactic attractions. Rohit would use his knowledge and the super computer to find any info he could about things. Jane and James would visit habitable planets. Anne would control the *Star Speeder* in her same pod if Michael had to use the space toilet, investigate planets he was interested in, or something important. Michael had the toughest job; being in charge of the *Star Speeder*, controlling it, making sure everything was right, and more. Every day, everyone would record in their virtual web cam logs on their super computers. Before they knew it, it was already March.

March 12 2011 AD- "Michael," James said through video chat on his super computer to Michael. "I think that we should head back to our own solar system now."

"Okay. We're only at the Alpha Centauri, the next closest star to Earth, so if I can make the super computer take us there in four light days, not light years, we should get there soon."

So, Michael converted the distance.

March 16 2011 AD- Earth came into the *Star Speeder's* view. *Zap!* "What was that?!" yelled Jane. *Zap!* "Ahh!" Rohit yelled. *Zap! Zap! Zap!* "Yikes," said James. Michael looked around, but didn't see anything. What was the whole commotion about? And what's that zapping sound? *Zap! Zap! Zap! Zap! Zap!* "Oh no, this is going to end up bad!" said Anne. Michael still hadn't seen it. He looked out of his window, and saw a flashing green light coming right towards him. "Ahh!" he yelled. "We're under attack!!!!!!!!!!" He closed his eyes, knowing that his life was probably over in seconds. *ZAP!*

Chapter 3
The LuAstrien Species

Michael opened his eyes. The laser had missed by an inch! He looked around rapidly, and saw something strange on the moon.

"Rohit," said Michael.

"Yes?" said Rohit.

"Can you please find out some information located on the *Star Speeder* database about the intergalactic location of that object on the moon?"

"No prob," Rohit began to type something on his super computer and finally found some data. "Uh, oh. I have a bad feeling about this."

"What?"

"It's at the Sea of Tranquillity. That's right where Apollo 11 had landed-the mission with the first man on the moon, James." The entire crew had been using video chat, and James seemed confused.

"Yikes! We better get there fast before any damage can be done!" Michael reduced the thrust and engaged the landing gear. Soon, the *Star Speeder* was on the moon. He pressed a red button and all the pod doors opened. When everyone was standing on the main floor, the top door opened, and the plank process started. Everyone got outside, and then the door locked.

They saw: aliens! A brown texture body, stretched head, and the same number of hands and legs as humans.

All the aliens fled, but a short one was too slow, and the crew surrounded it.

James picked him up by the neck. "Who are you and what do you want from us, our species, and the Earth?"

"I am part of the LuAstrien species," It said in a really low-pitched voice due to his choking. "If you want more information, I can't trust you, but I can give you a star map impossible for a dim-wit species, (like yours), to decipher."

"Well, where is it? Where's the star map?" asked Anne.

The alien showed a finger meaning that it would take a second or two. There seemed to be something coming up from his throat, as if he was about to vomit. Covered with this was something sort of round with some constellation diagrams on it.

Jane picked it up, and James took the alien to a little dungeon chamber where the crew would keep it prisoner while Rohit would investigate data on the alien.

Soon, the crew was on its way back towards Earth.

Rohit said to Michael, "Can you please turn on the auto-pilot feature and meet me upstairs?"

"Sure,' said Michael. He went up to the main area, and, like Rohit said, he found him there.

"Look at the star map," Rohit said.

"Okay, sure. Why?" Michael asked.

"They're stars, and I think they make up constellations."

"I think the whole crew knows that by now. Do you have something to add onto that?"

"Yes. I've been studying it for several hours now, and I came up with the idea that they'll make some sort of constellation, or constellations, in which we have to go there."

"So what's your point? Can you explain the idea more clearly?"

"Yes."

"Then please do."

"I thought that there might be an area of the constellations which we would have to go to to find the needed information on the LuAstrien species. The alien taught me how to pronounce the species name. It's (loo-aww-stree-in). But that's not all we need to know."

"So you investigated on all the known constellations to try to find which ones are on the star map?"

"Oh, yes. For two full hours. Then, I realized that they aren't constellations at all on the star map. It's a strategic problem. Trying to fool you. They're points that, when connected, will show us a clue. I'm 90% sure this time, but we need ultra-violet light to connect the dots."

As Rohit said "-ultra-violet light to connect the dots," Michael's eyes grew and he said "Come to my pod."

They did, and Rohit looked around the pod. "It's kinda' small in here." he finally commented.

"It only seems small because there are two people in it right now," Michael reassured him. Then, he sat on the chair and told him what to do. "First, hold it against the light. Now, stay there. I'm going to change the level of light in the pod from the visible light spectrum to the ultra-violet one." He strapped on some safety goggles and gave a pair to Rohit. "Wear these just in case the light harms your eyes."

Rohit put them on, and instantly resumed to holding the star map in front of the light. Michael changed the spectrum setting.

Some red lines began to form connecting the dots on the star map. "I think they're making a word, or a name," Rohit said. "E. R. I. S. *Eris!*" In capital letters, on the very star map that only a few minutes ago was only a bunch of stars was the single bunch of letter that made "Eris."

"Eris. *Eris.* Eris? What could that mean?" asked Rohit.

"Dunno," said Michael. "Hey. Do you think that it means the clue could be somewhere on the dwarf planet of Eris?"

"Maybe!" concluded Rohit. "Wait. Don't you think we should have noticed that before when we were flying past it on New Year's Day?"

"We were going at past light speed, remember? What you see means no sense if the light can't reach you! Besides, it shouldn't take much longer than a day to explore Eris with the *Star Speeder*. "

"Okay. Let's turn this thing around!"

"Wait a sec, Rohit! Wouldn't that be odd for the rest of the crew?"

"I guess...."

"You guessed right! Right before we go to sleep, I'll announce what we've just discovered, and then I'll set the *Star Speeder* on auto-drive."

"Okay. I guess that'll work out right."

"You're a good guesser, Rohit. You can go to your own pod now, and I'll change the light setting back to normal. See you later."

"Bye." Rohit said as he went back.

Later that day, Michael did as said. "It is now 10:30 pm Mountain Standard Time. That means it's time for you to go to hit the hay, but first, I want to share something. Me and Rohit were doing a little experiment, and found a clue pointing towards Eris- the not-as-famous dwarf planet past Pluto. So, we will be changing course. That's all for now. Good night, everyone."

He pressed the Auto-Drive button which brought up a search engine. He searched for Eris, which brought up a virtual 3-D model of it. He set the route for 100 kilometres above Eris, and then selected confirm.

Then, he pressed a button that lowered his chair headrest into a bed. His chair, along with everyone else's, could transform into something like that. In fact, he'd been doing so for the last of days. The lights dimmed. The pod became a much more comfortable-bedroom setting. Soon, he began to doze off....

Chapter 4
Eris and Nohanga's Story

He saw a cave, and at the rear of that cave were ruins he couldn't decode. The cave was barren. It seemed celestial somehow. Heavy breathing around him. He was being carried. Soon: a rumble. Dust. Something new appeared. You would see a corridor once the dust cleared, and two aliens from the LuAstrien species were currently walking down that corridor. Probably where the breathing was coming from. He saw an old human male walking with them. He was very bony. He was wearing nothing but a plain white vest and an undergarment. Apparently, he was quite hairy, as well. Wait a second-why was he in that shape? Was he literally in his shoes? Because that was who the LuAstriens were carrying.

Then, a voice which he couldn't find the source to began to speak, "No. No. No. Please, I beg of you, mercy!" His voice sounded poor, frightened and merciful. Wait-he was the one saying it! "Please."

A very deep voice with a mystery source-(Was it the LuAstrien on his left?)-replied. "No way shall we surrender. In your Earth Year 2011 AD, your wee, puny, little species and pathetic little planet will get pulverized!" The voice was full of loathe. "Mwah ha ha ha! In addition, you will stay here-to die!"

The first voice shouted, "Noooooooooooooooooo!"

"Noooooooooooooooooooooooooooooooooo!" screamed Michael. He then realized he was only in his *Star Speeder*. "Phew. It was just a dream. Well, it's nearly 8:30 anyways."

Then, he made out something small and circular out the Super-Computer window screen. It seemed rocky and icy. It was Eris!

"Let's search from a few metres above Eris. We'll land if we see something interesting." said Michael to the crew.

They did so for hours. At around the 4-Hour-Mark, they began to lose hope. But then, almost instantly, Anne spotted a cave. "A cave could be a perfect place to hide something-or someone." she concluded.

"You're right!" added Michael. "Though I don't know why it looks so familiar."

The *Star Speeder* landed, and everyone went outside with their baggy space suits on. They began to walk inside the cave, and every step closer Michael went closer to it, the more familiar it looked. When they reached the rear of the cave, the crew recognized runes in graffiti on the rear cave wall. To Michael, that too looked familiar.

"Uh, oh," stated Michael. "I can't decode runes. Well, actually I can, but I never learned how to decode an inscription like this."

"Neither can I." said Jane.

"Nor me." added Anne.

"Same here." sighed James.

"Looks like a dead end." concluded Michael.

"Wait!" yelled Rohit. Everyone's eyes turned to him. "I can!"

He got out a pen and notebook and began to decode. After a while, he figured it out.

"I got it!" he exclaimed. *"'Unscramble: terAroids.'*

"Look," said James. "I thought that we entered this cave to find a clue-not play a word problem."

For a couple seconds, Rohit gave James a cold hard stare. Finally, he said "Maybe this has something to do with it."

Rohit thought for a second.

"I think that it's 'Asteroid."

When he finished talking, the word "Asteroid" echoed throughout the cave. As that happened, the ground shook, and as *THAT* happened, the back cave wall began to sink down Eris' terrain.

When everything settled down, the crew noticed a corridor where the rear cave wall had been. It was also familiar to Michael, and the crew walked through the corridor.

Inside, he saw a bony man. It then hit him why it all looked familiar.

"WH-Who are you?" asked Anne, stammering.

"I am Nohanga"

"You-I-I dreamt about you," Michael said.

"Ahh-good. I sent a memory SOS throughout our galaxy. It's a good thing it was you and your brain who received the memory, and that it wasn't intercepted by a LuAstrien. Otherwise, I'd be dead by now!"

"But in the SOS dream-message-thing I intercepted from you, one of the LuAstriens said that you'd be left here to DIE, not SURVIVE. Right now, it looks you're doing just that: the complete opposite."

"That is because oxygen is a deadly gas for their species, but not to us Earthlings. LuAstriens go on Carbon Dioxide like a plant, but also Nitrogen and even no element like that. The chamber that you're in right now holds lots of oxygen. In fact-all the gasses humans need with just the right amount. Plus that cave wall was like an air lock. That way, the gasses here won't leave and the outside ones won't come in. The LuAstriens took this cave, made is shorter by adding a rock wall back there so that no one will know I'm here. You all look like a bunch of clever folk. Which one of you decoded those runes?"

Rohit put his hand up politely.

"So, now I suggest that you all can take your helmets off. You must be very uncomfortable from having to wear those blasted helmets on so long."

The crew removed their helmets. Nohanga was right. The sensation had been really irritating, and so now all this comfort was really a luxury. The crew smiled with delight.

"Is there anything you can tell us that we should know about the LuAstrien species?" inquired

Michael, because this is the reason that they came for.

"Listen carefully, because this is some information which hardly anyone on Earth knows about. The entire universe, for that matter. Feel honoured that I can trust you for such valuable information and data."

The crew's ears perched.

"Now, sit down, because this is a long story, younglings. Make sure you have nothing distracting you while I tell you this. Another thing before we continue is that I'll only repeat it once if not at all. It all began when...."

Chapter 5
"It All Began When"

"It all began when-"

"Sorry to interrupt, but how do you pronounce your name?" asked Jane.

"Well, no, like the opposite of yes. Hang, like you are hanging somewhere. A, like yelling 'Ahh!' No-hang-ah. Nohanga."

After a couple of tries, the crew got the hang of it. So, when everyone was settled down, he began to share his information with the crew.

"It all began when Neil Armstrong set foot on the moon. Well, if you're LuAstrien, you're a worker. The workers work for something on the moon-our moon-that no human knows about, except for one thing. The only thing I know about it is that it has its own worker, the co-leader. So, this mysterious thing is probably a leader, I guess. The co-leader makes sure all the workers are practically working their guts out. If someone is goofing off, or doing something that the co-leader isn't liking, the co-leader takes him or her to the mysterious thing, and then that LuAstrien regretted what he/she did, for that worker is never heard from again. This has happened very, very often throughout LuAstrien history. Think of it this way: three levels. The lowest level, which is made up of all the LuAstriens except for those which are the other levels, is a normal level. In human standard, it would be like being a slave. The next level, which there is only one of, is the Co-leader. That person would be in charge or all those other LuAstriens. But in charge of everyone is the Leader, who is some mysterious thing living on our moon. Oh, and another thing. LuAstriens never die of age. Also: I only know this because they kept me captive in a fake asteroid on the Kuiper Belt until now, when they brought me here to Eris.

Well anyways, the co-leader noticed that some life form was invading the moon. So, he raced to an asteroid in the Kuiper Belt that really isn't an asteroid. It's really a hollow camouflaged mass floating in space. It's like a planet for the LuAstrien species.

The co-leader told all the workers that Earth's moon was getting invaded. So, this called for panic. That was their previous home and the reason they temporarily had to live on this fraud asteroid. They decided that they would exterminate Earth in a decade or so. They've already started the process or preparation and are on their way to Earth.

The thing was, it took the co-leader a couple of decades finding the asteroid again, and actually getting back from the moon, so he had to announce it in 2001. That's good because it delayed it for thirty-two years."

"Wait a second," interrupted Michael. "If the LuAstrien have their own language, they were probably speaking in that. So then how come they could talk in English, then?"

"Good question. Not only did the LuAstriens train themselves in English, but also in Chinese, Hindi, German, French, Spanish, Nepalese, Arabic, Portuguese, Japanese, Korean, Philippine, Italian, Russian, in fact, any official language in the world! They would change whatever language they were speaking in pretty casually. Well, good question, Michael, but let's get back to the story.

After that, the co-leader noticed Neil Armstrong was the same life form as me, and I was kept at their highest security dungeon. They want to kill any and all

31

Earthlings unless they join forces with them, and I refused the terrible offer.

So, they took me to this cave on Eris which only the Chosen Few could find other that the LuAstrien species. I always wondered whom the Chosen Few would be, and if they would ever find me. Seems like you five are the Chosen Few, and you managed to succeed in the seemingly impossible mission to find me. You are the ones destined to save Earth from any extra-terrestrial harm.

However, now you'll have to find another way to gain more information if you ever wish to make an end to the terrible LuAstrien species. I have managed to gather some information on how you can gather any more information. Sorry, but this is all I know before they decided to "torture" me over here. Only the most clever could probably do it without the help of one, so try to find a LuAstrien, and present the Ancient Scroll to him or her."

"What's the Ancient Scroll?" all of the crew asked at the same time.

"Well, just like humans, the LuAstrien species has mythology. According to their mythology, the goddess Cornea was mad at the evil demon Retina for keeping who she loved hostage. So, she took out a scroll that was made at an industrial factory called "Rods & Cones". She dropped the scroll directly in Retina's hands. Retina looked at the scroll, but then its power began to crush Retina. So, Cornea married Pupil, who Retina had been keeping captive, and had a son named Optic Nerve who married someone named Iris. After the gods and goddesses died, for in their mythology they weren't immortal, it was said that the scroll is still floating around in the anti-gravity of outer space, which is where the battle between Cornea and Retina was held. I always thought it was pretty cool how all of their mythological names have to do with the parts of a human eyeball. Maybe that's where the eyeball parts originated from."

"Thanks for your time. Eris was once or is part of the Kuiper Belt according to most theories about it, so it won't take too long to find the scroll. Also, we have a LuAstrien kept in capacity. Okay, now come," said Michael.

"Come where?"

"With us, of course! It would be way better than staying on a deserted dwarf planet! We'll take care of you, and that's a promise!"

"I'm sorry, but I can't."

"Why not?"

"Sorry, but it's my job to pass my knowledge on to the world's next generation. If I die here, so be it."

"I'm sure we can reason it out, though."

"No need to. My decision is final. I'm staying."

"Don't you have any second thoughts about this?"

"If my decision wasn't final, I would possibly have made a second choice, young child."

"But-"

"No buts."

"Whatever. Well, we can't just leave you here!"

"No. I meant you don't start a sentence with the word 'but'. I've fulfilled my life's duties."

"This just doesn't seem right, Nohanga."

"I'm staying. Period."

"If this is the way you want it, okay. Bye. Let's go, guys."

As the crew left the cave, Nohanga's eyes stared at each other, and then his eyeballs went behind his eyes. Nohanga closed his eyes for the last time before passing away. Forever.

Chapter 6
To The Kuiper Belt

The crew approached their spacecraft. "I feel really bad for what we did," spoke Michael.

"It's for the best, and it's nature's way," said Anne, but she couldn't help crying and feeling bad for Nohanga. The last word Nohanga said was "period", for crying out loud!

Inside the *Star Speeder*, the crew discussed ways that they could use to retrieve the Ancient Scroll. Finally, they concluded that they would just have to search the whole Kuiper Belt as fast as they could.

"Hey-and we can split up, too!" added Michael.

"We can?" asked Anne.

"We can?" asked Jane.

"We can?" asked Rohit.

"We can?" asked James.

Michael could hardly believe that the whole crew didn't know that they could split up. So he said:

"Yeah; we can. We can't just go out there in our space suits! Then we'll only have a matter of hours to search the whole belt."

"Exactly," agreed Anne, Jane, and James together.

"That doesn't make any sense, Michael. One minute ago you're assuring us that we can split up to search the whole, vast Kuiper Belt. The next we know, you're telling us that we can't!" said Rohit after everyone else finished talking.

"No," corrected Michael. "Well, no **AND** yes. I'm sorry I was confusing you guys. I meant that we **CAN** split up, just that we can't do it in our space suits. In my pod, there are five 'Pod Unlock' buttons- four for you guys and one for me. When I press them, the five different pods unlock from the ten different metal bars. Then, we can steer ourselves to different places in the belt. I'm about to press the buttons. Is everyone ready?"

"Ready," agreed the whole crew at the same time. And with that, one by one, the different pods unleashed from their two metal bars.

Using the Super Computer's technology, they could still communicate and see each other, which was good just in case something unexpected that was bad happened.

They all discussed where they should all go to.

James' job was to search area three hundred and twelve.

Rohit's job was to search area five hundred and six.

Jane's job was to search area six hundred and fifty-two.

Anne's job was to search area eight hundred and eighty.

And last but absolutely not the least; Michael's job was to search area nine hundred and ninety-nine.

They all knew their areas pretty good because while their first discussion about the Kuiper Belt, Rohit was talking about O.S.A.C. That was short for "Outer Space Area Codes". There were trillions of trillions of trillions of trillions of trillions of area codes! A little thing he'd come up with. There were one thousand in the Kuiper Belt. They discussed the ones most likely to hold the Ancient Scroll, the least likely to hold the Ancient Scroll, and the ones that fit in neither category. At the end, there were only two in the "likely" category and two in the "least likely" category. They decided to search the least likely because sometimes the best place to find something is where you probably won't.

In the second discussion, they found Michael had no area code to go to. He took the "least likely" one step higher. He selected one that fit in neither category. There was just something about area code number nine hundred ninety-nine that made him just want to search it right away.

So as I was saying, the crew split up.

June 5 2011 AD- After a couple of weeks, everyone reached their areas. All of the areas except for Michael's have a weird sign on a nearby asteroid that was in their area. No one could make any sense out of the signs.

James began to communicate to the crew.

"Guys-an asteroid over here is really bright as if it is an incandescent light bulb. Though weirder yet: there are really dark marks on it that looks like skull and crossbones though the skull doesn't seem human."

"Let me see, James," Rohit said.

"Here."

Rohit examined for a while then said:

"Looks like the skull of a LuAstrien. It's actually trying to say a number: 506. But what does that mean?"

"Maybe it's some sort of code," Jane said.

"That's right. Though what kind of code could it be is the question…," Anne said.

"It's probably a code that will help guide us to the Ancient Scroll," Michael added.

"Well, obviously," Jane said, rolling her eyes,

"Maybe I should get a closer look, don't you think?" James asked.

"And since when were we stopping you from doing that?" Anne pointed out.

James flew his pod closer to the asteroid; approaching cautiously.

Suddenly, right before his eyes, the asteroid grew at a rapid pace, turning into something reminding him of the Death Star from Star Wars. Just more yellow-ish and resembling a face.

It was a sphere with thousands of tiny lasers, a line of medium-sized lasers, and one humongous laser. Its gravity clutch was so big, it was pulling James's pod towards it at one million kilometres per second! The pod lost all contact with the rest of the crew. James tried to break free of the clutch using techniques that he learnt from training at the Astronomical Voyagers Academy, but the clutch was just too strong. The pod crash-landed at the top of the sphere. There were tall lines there that felt like hair all around the pod. James rolled out of the broken pod and stood up with difficulty. His legs were bleeding and some blood was dripping down to his left shoe from his cheek. One of the lines picked up James and dropped him at the ground a couple of times, as if they were real. Another line fixed the pod enough to go back in space. The line that was hurting James moved him into the pod and launched it far into space.

It was rolling at a rapid pace through the very, *very* thin atmosphere around the intergalactic sphere that was neither a planet nor a dwarf planet. James was feeling really nauseous when the pod stopped spinning and felt like he was about to vomit. Suddenly, the humongous laser took the form of a nose while the line took the form of a mouth.

It was an alien monster!

* * * * *

The monster began to chase the pod. James couldn't go as fast as the monster, though he still had enough power to run away from it. He sighed with relief when he found out that one of the pod's external lasers was working. He shot about a thousand times at the monster.
No impact.
Then, the thousands of small lasers, the mouth lasers, and the nose laser shot at him.

38

James felt so weak that he almost went unconscious.

This is the end. James thought as a single tear went down his cheek. *No one will ever know what happened to me. It'll be a mystery forever. Earth will get invaded by LuAstriens.* All the lasers were nearly done charging for enough power to kill James. *Well, nice knowing me.*

The lasers were getting ready to shoot at the pod.

Then, suddenly, James got an idea. The monster had no eyes! It probably hunted by movement. So he found a piece of crushed metal and threw it far into space. The monster chased after it. James saw that there were no lasers on the back. So he found some spare parts and built a laser. He shot about what seemed like a million times at it.

It exploded.

A weird hissing sound was coming as that happened. He sort of heard some words in his mind:

Rohit Tracking System Area Code Number Five Hundred and Six.

His eyes began to drift off and closed. Then everything went black.

Absolutely black.

* * * * *

"James. James. WAKE UP!!!!!!!!!!!!!" a voice said.

Immediately, he opened his eyes.

"Are you okay?" asked Michael.

"Yeah…. What happened to me?" asked James.

"We found you floating through space unconscious. Your pod had-"

"Had what?"

"It-Oh, I don't know how to say it."

"What? Say what? What happened to my pod?"

"Your pod is destroyed. I'm sorry, James. But Rohit is an excellent engineer. He reconstructed your pod, but it will never be the same."

"Thanks, Rohit. But where are we, Michael?"

"Inside the *Star Speeder*. We decided it would be safest to go around space together. Anyways-what happened after your connection turned off?"

So James explained about everything. Then he explained about the hissing sound. Jane said that they *had* to go to Rohit's area.

"Maybe certain area codes have clues we need to find the scroll," Anne said "So let's find it? To Area Code 506!"

* * * * *

"Wow." Michael gasped. The whole area was covered by one huge asteroid. The crew approached. Suddenly, the asteroid's craters turned into eyes, a nose, and a mouth. It began to talk. It breathed fire whenever it finished a word.

"Select the asteroid with number two.

The one that seems O' strong and true.

40

In a place that starts with a six.

Now make a deposit of fifty two fire mint sticks."

"Fire mint sticks?" asked Rohit. "Even *I* haven't heard of that!"

"Hold on," said Michael. "It was fiction with fun kid recipes which 'aliens would love'. It always seemed childish, but worth a shot! I've got a book entitled *'Alien Foods'*."

The face-alien-monster didn't want to wait. It began to attack the *Star Speeder* with fire. Luckily, it's nearly fire proof. But it takes a few minutes to recharge. If exposed to too much fire and not enough time to recharge, it may burn. So Michael didn't have much time.

After some hard work, he managed to find a one hundred page chapter about fire treats. He started looking through it. Finally, at page nine hundred ninety-nine, he found a page about fire mint sticks. It said that to create it, you need to chant the Acciotambara spell. Finally, he managed to do it just right. Suddenly, some fire mint sticks appeared in his hand. He threw them through space. It landed in one of the mouth craters. The craters started to swallow it. Then, it exploded into a million pieces.

* * * * *

"We have to solve the riddle." said Rohit.

"Don't you guys get it?" Jane asked. "Fire mint sticks were originated in my area. There were six batches of fifty-two fire mint sticks. We have to search area six hundred fifty two!

* * * * *

July 26 2011 AD-Finally, they all arrived at area six hundred fifty two. There was ANOTHER huge asteroid. As soon as they got there, it started to dissolve. Then, it was gone. Vanished.

"Hmm," Jane commented after several long, silent minutes. "That's weird."

"What's weird?" questioned Anne.

"I was expecting it to turn into a monster or something like that."

The crew was quiet for one minute while they were thinking.

And another minute.

And another and another and another minute!

The crew began to doze off without knowing it. Their mind probably just needed it.

Suddenly, it felt like something was pulling the *Star Speeder* towards it using its gravitational clutch. Then the crew saw it. It was a nightmare come true.

"Oh, no!" shouted Michael.

It must have been what the asteroid turned into.

42

He desperately tried to break through the clutch using techniques from training, but it was of no use.

Michael then tried a trillion other things. Also of no use. Infact, it made it worse. All electricity disappeared. The engine flew into what the asteroid had turned into.

The *Star Speeder* was falling into a **BLACK HOLE**!!!!!!!!!!!!!!!!!!!!!!!

Chapter 7
Inside Another Dimension

"AHHHHHHHHHHHHHHH!!!!!!!!!!!!" yelled the crew. They finally got sucked inside the black hole.

FLASH!

It felt as if they had stopped breathing. It felt as if their hearts had stopped pounding. It felt as if all their memory had escaped from their brain. It felt as if they were dying and coming back to life-several times over. It felt as if every time they were reborn they and the universe changed a bit. The *Star Speeder* exploded and rebuilt itself. The universe seemed as if it was a swirl spinning 360 and never stopping.

FLASH!

Finally, after what seemed like a million years, the *Star Speeder* popped out in a universe that is symmetric to ours but somehow different. They were in a parallel universe. A whole other dimension.

* * * * *

The crew freaked out. It was a really traumatic experience. They had never felt anything like.

Imagine the scariest roller coaster ride combined with one of those rides when you drop from sky and are bumped again, times a trillion. Then, you might have even touched the idea of this experience.

Apparently, it had done something with their minds as well.

The crew had gone crazy, started yanking on wires, and, pretty much, were acting like a bunch of wild animals.

"Guys," Michael said. "First things first. I know that this is really weird. That's not really that important right now. But what's really that important now right now is to try and find a way back to the other side of the black hole."

Rohit sighed.

"Your right. Wait a sec-because we're on this side of the black hole, we've lost all communication with the other side of the black hole," said Rohit. "But our *Star Speeder's* built-in connection still works! I'll try and find something helpful on my super computer."

So, he began typing away and opened a file.

"Guys-listen to this," he said. So he began reading the rest of the crew members the file. "'You know the theory of how the universe started with the Big Bang? Before that, it was just trillions of trillions of things bunched together so that it was the size of an atom, right. And then some great force banged next to it and the atom-sized thing began expanding to form the universe. And most astronomers believe that it is still expanding today. They also believe something even more complicated. All we can predict about the universe so far is that the universe started out the size of an atom. But what was-and is-around the universe? Other collections of collections of stars that started the size of atoms? That's what some astronomers believe. Because what if the same thing happened to other atoms? If this theory is true, these collections of collections of stars are together a group called the multiverse. The different collections of collections of stars are like universes. I mean, you know that everything is located in something else. Like your house is in your neighborhood in your community in your city in your state or province in your country in your continent on your planet in your solar system in your galaxy in your star cluster in your universe-but then it just stops. What is the universe in? The multiverse! Then it would just be something else of what THAT is located in. Some even say that they are different dimensions that are symmetric to each other but still somehow different and are linked together by special portals: black holes. Like a parallel universe, basically.'"

"Great!" said James happily, but he was just being sarcastic. Then, he switched to a much different voice. "Now tell us what all that means!"

"I *did*. Anyways, it means that the black hole was a sort of portal that took us to another dimension! So, if we want to go back, we just have to go back through!"

* * * * *

So, with all their might, the crew tried to go back through the black hole. Though it was as if some invisible force wasn't letting it through.

The only effect was a bunch of other sucked-in material coming to the dimension, and they had nothing to do with it.

"Wow," said Jane. "I didn't know that a black hole was an intergalactic one-way."

46

Then the crew began trying to find another way. Soon, they came up with a theory.

Rohit thought that if black holes were portals linking up universes, they had to search this dimension to find another black hole that took them to the universe they'd started their mission in.

Michael thought something else, sort of an after effect, but only he believed in it. Everyone else believed Rohit's theory.

So, they began to wander off searching for other black holes. Rohit said that most astronomers believe that there is a super black hole at the center of most galaxies, including the Milky Way. Rohit said that he didn't believe it though. He said there are more small galaxies than big galaxies, so there was a better chance finding one in a small one. He said that the thing at the center of the Milky Way might be a LuAstrien stronghold.

Michael though Rohit had lost his mind in the previous dimension.

So, the crew decided to go to Galaxy Rohit 1. It was a galaxy that Rohit had found through the telescope in their room at the Astronomical Voyagers Academy. When he tried to tell everyone there, only Team Ten believed him at first. Rohit said that there was a lot of activity in the center of Galaxy Rohit 1, and it seemed like a black hole. It was the smallest galaxy ever discovered.

August 10 2011 AD-The crew got to Galaxy Rohit 1. It was pretty far from the Milky Way, though when Rohit discovered it, the galaxy was very close to the Milky Way. They all agreed it was just because they were in another dimension-even Michael agreed. Though in this dimension, the *Star Speeder* would go way *faster* than light speed!

"Okay," said Rohit. "According to," James completely lost track of whatever "Scientific Mumbo Jumbo" Rohit was talking about. "So, if I'm correct, it would cause a corruption at the opposite end of the electromagnetic spectrum causing the special type of black hole to activate which will make nearby material sucked in and dimensions will collide and so whatever material is close to the black hole in both dimensions will switch dimensions and so the aftermath would be that we arrive in-

"Now what language are you speaking?" rudely interrupted James.

"-our original dimension. You know, maybe it's *you* who doesn't understand English then. Anyways, it should be easy to find the black hole."

* * * * *

August 11 2011 AD-They all arrived at the black hole. On Rohit's command, with all his might, Michael steered the *Star Speeder* through the black hole.

"AHHHHHHHHHHHHHHH!!!!!!!!!!!" yelled the crew. They finally got sucked inside the black hole.

It felt as if they had stopped breathing. It felt as if their hearts had stopped pounding. It felt as if all their memory had escaped from their brain. It felt as if they were dying and coming back to life-several times over. It felt as if every time they were reborn they and the universe changed a bit. The *Star Speeder*

48

exploded and rebuilt itself. The universe seemed as if it was a swirl spinning 360 and never stopping.

Chapter 8
Michael's Theory

They popped out of the black hole. But it had seemed as if nothing had changed. In fact, nothing had changed.

"I just don't get it," said Rohit. "We came out of the black hole which we first came through. We should've been taken back to the universe we started our mission in-or at least in a different dimension. But we are in the same one even after going through! What can we do now?"

"Well," Michael said. "Why not we try doing it according to *my* theory now?"

Everyone except Rohit was willing to try it. So they all huddled in a group and Michael discussed the plan.

"I think that we should travel to the center of the Milky Way," said Michael. "I for one think that a black hole might be there. And I read a book – a non-fiction one – that suggested that some black holes might give a traveler some sort of option that would let you pick your destination from some choices."

"So? What about it?" asked Rohit in a rude manner.

"It means that the destinations are different dimensions. There's a big chance that one of the dimensions might be the one we wish to go to. If not, we could always try another large galaxy. For example, the Andromeda Galaxy."

Everyone thought it was a good idea except Rohit. He probably thought the plan was good, but right now, he was envious of Michael. Before Michael knew it, he too was against Rohit. They suddenly became rivals. All throughout their journey to the center of the galaxy, they both got into constant arguments, and the rest of the crew had to keep them calm, which was very tough. Usually during rides to places in their mission, Michael would ask Rohit information about several things. During this one, he didn't ask Rohit anything. For the rest of the crew, it was non-stop madness.

August 15 2011 AD-They arrived at the center of the galaxy. The *Star Speeder* had been set on auto-drive and everyone was deep in sleep, and Anne, Jane, and James woke up to a wonderful sound.

"Ahhhhhhhhhhhh!!"

It seemed to be coming from Michael's pod. They opened the door.

"Ahhhhhhhhhhhhhhhhhhh!!!!!!!!!!!!!!!!!!!!!!!!"

They saw Rohit inside the pod with Michael with a mischievous smile on his face.

"Ahhhhhhhhhhhhhhhhhhhhh!!!!!!!!!!!!!!!!!!!!!!!!!!!!!!!" Michael was yelling. He then pointed at Rohit, and for the first time, they saw an odd device in his hand. "He electrocuted me!"

"What?" said Anne, Jane, and James at the same time.

"I did nothing!" stammered Rohit, but it wasn't very convincing.

"What did you do?" asked James.

"Nothing!"

"Don't lie! What did you do?" exclaimed Jane.

"Nothing-I swear!"

Anne whispered something to Jane and James that sounded like: "I have an idea."

"Don't listen to them," said Anne. "Hey-what's that thing you're holding?"

"Well, I spent all of last night trying to make something to capture attention with electricity by serving out a non-harmful electric shock. You just have to hold it in your non-dominant hand to send electricity through your body. Then, you'd touch someone and they get full attention on it. So I tried it out on Michael. It (luckily) didn't work out well causing him to get electro-"

Rohit had just realized what he was saying.

"So you admit it!"

Rohit glared at Michael, who glared back. They gnashed their teeth. Before they knew it, they were fighting and shouting at each other.

"Stop it, guys!" shouted Anne and broke up the fight. "We're there!"

They all felt a jerk and seemed to be hurtling towards something.

"Quick, guys," said Michael. "Imagine really hard about the Earth from our dimension!"

"Why should I listen to *him*?" asked Rohit.

"On second thoughts, you shouldn't listen to me. Then you can stay trapped in this dimension and save a lot of trouble for everyone!" Michael then let out a maniacal laugh.

"FINE! I'LL DO IT!" shouted Rohit, but didn't feel very thrilled about it.

"AHHHHHHHHHHHHHHH!!!!!!!!!!!" yelled the crew. They finally got sucked inside the black hole.

It felt as if they had stopped breathing. It felt as if their hearts had stopped pounding. It felt as if all their memory had escaped from their brain. It felt as if they were dying and coming back to life-several times over. It felt as if every time they were reborn they and the universe changed a bit. The *Star Speeder* exploded and rebuilt itself. The universe seemed as if it was a swirl spinning 360 and never stopping.

Chapter 9
"What The?"

The *Star Speeder* exited a black hole. They popped out of the Andromeda Galaxy.

"What the?" said Michael in James voice. "We're in the same dimension, but in a different galaxy! Why would that happen?"

The crew began to think-well most of them.

Michael, Anne, Jane, and James suddenly heard Rohit whistling.

"Ugh," said Michael. "How could I be so dumb? Rohit knows how to trigger images in people's minds without them realizing it! Why didn't I realize that?"

"Rohit-don't trigger our minds this time," said Jane. "Please-for me."

Rohit immediately agreed. They had developed a love interest. Michael and Anne also had a love interest. Though I think this is better for another time.

"Okay guys," said Michael. "Put the image of Earth into your mind." Everyone did so.

Starting at a slow pace, the *Star Speeder* inched a little closer. Then, the gravity of the black hole began sucking the *Star Speeder* towards it as if it was a tornado that started out minor but ended up with a huge amount of wind.

"AHHHHHHHHHHHHHHH!!!!!!!!!!!" yelled the crew. They finally got sucked inside the black hole.

It felt as if they had stopped breathing. It felt as if their hearts had stopped pounding. It felt as if all their memory had escaped from their brain. It felt as if they were dying and coming back to life-several times over. It felt as if every time they were reborn they and the universe changed a bit. The *Star Speeder* exploded and rebuilt itself. The universe seemed as if it was a swirl spinning 360 and never stopping.

* * * * *

This time, instead of coming out of a black hole, the *Star Speeder* grew out from some space debris near the Earth. Their voices had become normal again.

The date was January the first. 2011. Then, their whole mission re-happened. All the way until the part when they were discussing about the fire mint riddle. Jane told everyone that they shouldn't go to her area, and instead, head to Anne's.

August 26 2011 AD-They arrived at the area Anne had been assigned to. They then heard some rasping voices. It sounded as if it was trying to point out a number.

"What's that sound?" asked Jane.

"It seems distinctly LuAstrien...," replied Rohit. "Hang on-I've got a book called '*LuAstrien Numbers*' that the LuAstrien we are keeping captive threw up one day."

"Who's stopping you from reading it?" said Jane with a smirk on her face.

Rohit began reading. He finally found out what the number was.

"The number is 999!" he finally announced. "According to the pattern of clues, that must mean that we should head to Michael's area!"

As soon as he finished talking, the voices became deadly and painful.

"We have to get away from the voices *now*!" said Anne, and James nodded in agreement before he said:

"Wait-where's Michael?"

Chapter 10
The Ancient Scroll
Part 1

The crew searched around the *Star Speeder* and then noticed that even the LuAstrien was missing.

"The LuAstrien might have something to do with Michael's disappearance." said Anne.

They continued searching the *Star Speeder* for a while. Then, suddenly, when Anne walked past the cage in which the crew was keeping the LuAstrien captive, she noticed blood was on a concrete wall right next to the cage. It made out many signs that seemed like a cross between the Greek alphabet and ancient runes like at the cave on Eris. She got Rohit to meet her there.

"Why should I do it?" Rohit said in a raised voice. "I *hate* Michael. You are about as smart as the dumbest creature that has ever lived in the multiverse if you have not realized that yet. And I advise you not to like Michael either."

"But I like him!" Anne fired back at him. Then she turned red. But that's not the point. What the point really is is that we need to save him! He is the captain of this vessel. Have you not heard of the saying about the captain and his ship?"

"Of course I have. I'm a genius-remember?"

"You are such a-. So are you doing it or not?"

"Of course not! That's ridiculous!"

"But you're the only one who can decode ancient runes and any language, for that matter. And that includes Ancient Greek!"

"I still won't do it. Unless....,"

"Unless what?"

"Unless you promise that after we decipher the runes and find Michael that you will stop liking him."

Anne took a moment to let that all soak in. She didn't want to not like Michael. However, that means that Rohit wouldn't decipher the ancient runes and that they would never find Michael. And how would she ever see him again, then? What should she do? She kept on thinking for a while and finally thought of the right option.

"I promise."

"Excellent."

Rohit took out his notebook and a pencil from his side pocket. He started jotting some notes down. A little after that, he did a gesture with his head that told Anne it would take a while and that she should just leave and do whatever she wanted.

* * * * *

Later that day, Anne was sipping some coffee in the *Star Speeder* lounge which was located at the left side of the main area. She was reading a paperback novel called *"The End of Cartabania"*. It was one of her favourite science-fiction books of all time. It was about an unnamed species of aliens that

58

could take people of great power to a planet called Cartabania. In it, a crew member from a five-manned crew was lost and the rest of the crew took off to find them and end the alien species and their jail planet where the crew suspected he was being held captive. Then all of a sudden, Rohit rushed into the door and started talking.

"It said 'Jefferson, Michael has been space napped by the LuAstrien. To find him, visit the planet stating with a C and ends with an A. It shall be the location of this planet hidden too well for humans. Wait a second-let me see that book, please."

Anne first hesitated. Then, she handed the book to Rohit. He opened the book and quickly flipped through. After reading the back cover, he turned the book back over to the front cover. He did a quick scan for the author's name, though didn't find it. So he turned to the copyright page and saw that the author's name was Al U. E. Srint.

"An uncommon name," Rohit finally remarked. "More, I think he should be more foreign than anyone's vision of foreign. I think his imaginarium is something no human-or species on Earth-could have thought of."

"Rohit," Anne said with a puzzled face. "What are you talking about?"

"Try scrambling-or as I should say-*un*scrambling his name."

Anne closed her eyes and imagined the letters that formed the author's name, and then moved them around.

"LuAstrien," she breathed. "Though what does that prove?"

"What's the book about?"

She quickly explained.

"Cartabania," Rohit began. "Is real."

Anne's jaw dropped open.

"Well," started Rohit, knowing that she was about to ask what he was talking about. He yawned. "I'm kind of tired. Nothing like a good, nice, long rest to get the old, dusty gears turning."

Anne could tell that Rohit was just trying to change the subject, but decided that she was also tired. All of a sudden, they heard a fire alarm blaring. James came bursting from his pod, barely able to breathe.

"There was fire...," James panted. "A shadow...letters in – Guh, huh, huh"

He was so tired that he fainted, so Rohit and Anne knew it was serious. Rohit went to find Jane, and he found her sleeping in her pod. No matter how much Rohit shook her, she would not wake.

Meantime, Anne went to find the *Star Speeder's* special anti-gravity space fire extinguisher. A few short minutes later, the fire was gone. The fire extinguisher, now in Rohit's hand, dropped to the floor with a THUD. Rohit saw the message that James was talking about. It was Greek and Arabic. He could tell since it included letters such as Ω, $\sum$, Ψ, Δ, ـص, ع, and غ. He could also tell that it was in English, just in the

Greek or Arabic lettering system. The message is on the page of this book right after the story.

Rohit went to Jane's pod, picked her up, and plopped her on one of the lounge's recliners around the small, circular table that Anne was sitting in before since it was no longer safe in their pods.

When Rohit got back to the lounge, Anne picked up James by the ear and dragged him onto another one of the recliners. Rohit and Anne then also sat down. Soon, they could hear that James was coming to since he was making soft snores. He then woke up with a start.

"Wha-?" James said. "Oh – I – Um- I – Maybe fainted."

"Yes, James." Anne said, shifting her weight. "What were you talking about when you mentioned a shadow? Can you maybe describe it?"

"Well, I don't remember exactly. But what I *do* remember is that the shadow – it just might have all been in my head – but it seemed to resemble that of a LuAstrien. Though it was more of a silhouette – it didn't belong to anyone."

Anne and Rohit exchanged faces, though when they turned back, they saw that James was snoring again – this time, **MUCH** louder. Anne turned to face Rohit so that they could exchange non-serious, grinning faces, but instead, she found Rohit also snoozing. Anne muttered something about men, but before she knew it, she too was fast asleep.

* * * * *

"Shauakashushilafasatopasayooshisushi"

Whispers that made no sense and sounded like that were being spoken in the air. Though there was no source to the voices, as if the air was speaking. It managed to make its way into Anne's mind. When it reached, it almost sounded painful.

Anne woke with a start. She was breathing heavily. She then mistakenly thought that the voices were from her imagination-and remember, *mistakenly.*

Though she could still hear soft voices, she decided that it might have been James', still snoring loudly, snoring.

It   was   not   that   at   all.

Finally, Anne decided to wake up. However, she was so tired that, before she got out of her recliner, she dropped back in her seat and she fell asleep   again   like   a   rock.
Her dreams from that moment on were very dark and she kept on hearing the nonsense whispers. Over time, the whispers started to seem like English, though she wasn't sure if she understood the mysterious whisper-language or if they themselves were   starting   to   speak   in   English.
Then, because of what Anne heard, she was terrified. The whispers kept on repeating cuss words and talked about the different, cruel tortures that were happening to....

Anne woke with a start. She was too shocked to register the fact that she could still hear the whispers. When she finally registered it, the whispers continued   as   absolute   nonsense.

She decided to wake up and started, even though she was still half asleep, searching around the *Star* *Speeder*.

She came back where she had started. The search had proved unsuccessful. She still had not found the source of the mysterious voices.

She then decided to go back to sleep. Just before she was about to drift away, something kept her back from lying down in her recliner.

It was not the type of feeling that seems like there is something invisible there; it was a feeling like something was watching you. Anne did not want to give up. So, she got back up. She started to walk in a random direction. This was because that she was still half asleep. Almost at the stage of sleep-walking.

However, after what happened next, she was not at all still half asleep.

She found herself at the door of the gigantic pantry. She opened the door.

* * * * *

She saw a dark, scary seeming figure.

The figure seemed familiar. Only later did she know where she had seen it before. In fact, she couldn't recall why that figure was familiar.

She did not dare approach any closer. When she opened the pantry door, even though she couldn't see the silhouette, an odd, cold sensation told her that the silhouette had heard the creak of the door.

* * * * *

"Now that we have gotten rid of Jefferson, we can kill the other Earthlings aboard that horrid *Star Speeder*. Now, it will be the time for *their* downfall. Soon, we shall rule the entire universe at the dominant species!" Whispers from the silhouette were saying. Though since it didn't seem like the word "whisper" should be in plural form, Anne could've sworn that there was someone else in the pantry other than Anne and the silhouette. The thought made her shiver in fear. She had never been anywhere as brave as Michael. Nor as smart. What had the silhouette meant by "dominant species"? She had heard that humans were the dominant species on *Earth* but never a certain planet's being group, such as Earth's being Earthlings, and, if there were, Mars' being Martians, be a dominant species in the entire *universe.* And maybe there were even dominant species in the entirety of the *multiverse*! What could all this mean? There was no such thing!

The silhouette continued, "No one can get to Cartabania! It is not only lost in space-it is lost in time."

Then she heard a new voice, which explained why it sounded like the person-or alien-was talking to someone other than itself. The new voice sounded harsh, but it almost sounded afraid in a way. While she was thinking about the new voice, she realized something about the old voice. It was familiar. However, she just didn't know from where she remembered it from. The new voice, on the other hand, as harsh as it did sound, it was cackling. Not the laugh sort of cackling-it seemed as if the new voice was almost afraid. Judging by the silhouette, the new voice's body was a hunchback. Though it was not like any hunchback that you might see on Earth-so this one was also an alien. The other silhouette, which before Anne thought was also an alien, actually began to seem human. She just could not find out why. The new voice said, "Ma-ma-master, where is it found?"

The other voice laughed and then replied, "We don't know, of course! Do you have a point?"

"Th-th-then when J-J-Jefferson was taken there-how did we...."

"Know then but not now? It keeps changing position throughout all dimensions. Surely *you* all people should know what they are, now shouldn't you, my young *genius*?"

The hunchback stood up to him-figuratively AND literally, "A-a-are you *mocking* me?"

The more humanoid figure's voice became sterner, "Speak wisely, little one. You do **not** want to face *my* wrath. Just tell me the five dimensions."

"The first one is forward and backwards. The second dimension is left and right. The third is up and down. Number four is time. The last one, the fifth dimension is...."

"Yes?"

"I-I-I don't know."

"I don't know, *sir*."

"I-I don't know, sir."

"Very well. The first four dimensions are correct. You know *them*. Then why is it that you don't know the last one? Is it because you really *do* want to face my wrath?"

"N-n-no, sir. It's just that I thought that only the Earthlings use it, and this must not be true. We should not care about *our* gods. They are just the first LuAstrien beings. And our *true* god-is you. Th-th-the Earthlings, however, think that the fifth dimension is *their* religion god. Or gods, for some of their religions."

"Yes, the Earthlings believe that the fifth dimension is god, or gods in some cases. Divinity, basically. This is not true. It's just a religious belief even with them. Also-I don't know why it is that you believe that they have civilizations. Human Beings are so undeveloped, so prehistoric-like, that it is impossible for them to actually have *real* civilizations."

"Then what *is* the fifth dimension, my master?"

"The fifth dimension, silly LuAstrien is gr...."

Both silhouettes turned around. They must have realized that Anne was there. The humanoid silhouette's voice suddenly became very stern, deep, and felt mechanical, **"KILL THE EAVESDROPPER!"**

At first, the LuAstrien silhouette hesitated, but then, out of nowhere, picked up a weapon like no other.

This weapon, which was an ovalish machine that spun around, had a single strap that looked like a gun's strap. The LuAstrien clicked it, and a greenish, eye-blinding laser shot out of it. It destroyed everything its path. A huge stack of chemistry beakers, test tubes and chemicals smashed to floor and   disintegrated.

Anne then did what just about anyone would do   in   that   sort   of   situation. She   ran.

After a few minutes running around the *Star Speeder* like crazy, Anne stopped so she could breathe. The LuAstrien figure was hot on her trail. He (the LuAstrien looked like a male) was catching up with Anne so fast that she had not even started running   again   when   he   arrived.

Anne turned around and started to run again. But   it   was   no   use.

Once Anne reached the weaponry closet, the LuAstrien figure picked up his weapon and was about to   use   it   when:

Anne sealed her eyes shut. She then opened it about five seconds later when she realized two things:

1. The LuAstrien was the one that the crew was holding captive until he escaped!
2. She could get a weapon from the closet!

The LuAstrien shot his ray at Anne!

Just in time, Anne summersaulted away, and the ray hit the glass closet instead.

While the *Star Speeder's* alarms were blaring and red was flashing all throughout the craft, Anne used this new opportunity to pick up a weapon. With some quick moves, she summersaulted back to the now-smashed glass see-through window covering 90% of the closet. She quickly picked up a random weapon.

When she got back up on her feet, she saw what "weapon" she had picked up through the red light.

It was a plastic dart gun.

How could she use *that* to injure a LuAstrien? Would it even delay the movements of the once-captive LuAstrien?

She took just a second too long pondering upon those questions.

The LuAstrien came even closer to Anne. Its ray was put in ready position. One of its greasy fingers was just ahead of the ray's strap.

Anne had no choice. She either had to use the plastic dart gun or face her end. Naturally, she had to shoot using her "weapon".

What happened next was beyond the ordinary.

WAY beyond.

It felt as if the darts which she had just shot were going in slow motion.

When they hit the LuAstrien, celestial green rope spurt out from the back of all the darts. They intertwined, connected, and removed from some darts to form a huge rope. Then, as if it were magic, the humongous rope tied around the LuAstrien figure. All of a sudden, duct tape appeared out of nowhere and, as if the air was doing it, sealed the LuAstrien's mouth.

All this happened in less than five seconds.

* * * * *

After her midnight adventure, Anne decided to continue sleeping. The thing was-it wasn't a midnight adventure:

As soon as Anne settled back in her recliner, she heard a couple of yawns.

Anne, with wrinkles under her eyes, squinted at a digital clock hanging on the wall.

It was morning.

Before she knew it, Anne, so tired that she could barely speak, was explaining her adventure to James.

She didn't tell Rohit. She was afraid it would interfere a little bit with her decision in exchange for Rohit's service to decode the message.

However, it was very hard to keep it secret from Rohit.

When Rohit had woken up seeing the craft trashed and Anne looking as if she had been up all night, well, let's just say that he got a *little* suspicious.

Even if Anne could still keep it a secret, she

couldn't do that forever.

Rohit was the only one other than Anne than knew about the reality of Cartabania. This just *had* to have something in relation. The night's adventure and Cartabania-it just felt like there was some connection.

Anne was so tired that she could barely remember whether or not the LuAstrien and other figure actually *had* mentioned something about Cartabania.

If so, then what was it?

Then, she realized something.

Jane.

Where was she again?

In her pod!

What had happened last night right before Anne's adventure?

After all that had happened, it was hard to remember. Luckily, she finally did.

Once she did, a new puzzle piece about Michael being lost was collected: Last night, James had seen a weird figure-that must be the LuAstrien! Rohit had tried to wake Jane up, but she was in too deep a sleep.

Anne rushed to Jane's pod to find her still fast asleep. She shook Jane's shoulder in order to hear a groaning "what?" as the end result.

Jane sat up and turned her body towards Anne, who was standing on the right side of her. As she had planned, Anne told Jane all about her midnight adventure. Then, she added, "What do you know about this incident?"

Jane replied, "Your description of the two figures fit perfectly with a previous encounter which I can recall from my memory."

"Really? You did? What?"

"Yeah-I remember two figures-why is it so hard

to remember? Oh, yeah-those two figures, they, um…. They forced me to d-d-drink this potion-thing in some sort of…ugh! Um-it was in some sort of beaker. So I had to drink it, and the effects were-what were they again? Oh-so that's why."

"What was it? 'So that's why' what?"

"Once I drank the weird, potion-thingamajig, I sort of fell asleep and the reason why it's so hard to remember what had happened is because one of the effects of the potion-thingamajig is that I would have lost memory of the incident."

"Then how come you can remember what had happened *now*?"

"I think that the effects are starting to wear off."

Anne lowered her voice, "Do you think that this might have anything to do with Michael?

"Well, duh!"

"Well, that was very reassuring."

With that, before Jane could say anything else, Anne left the pod in silence.

* * * * *

That night, though Anne dreaded falling asleep, she could find no other choice. She dreamt of two dreams-one of Nohanga and one of her previous night's adventure.

In the one of Nohanga:

The "dream" was more audio than video-she heard Nohanga's voice, but she saw nothing but complete blackness. She wondered if this was Nohanga's spirit after death that was part of some external subconscious-almost like rebirth with the same soul of the previous, main/root conscious-Nohanga himself.

She heard, words coming from Nohanga, "The LuAstriens have control over memory-their presence

70

by itself could cause short term memory loss or simply to forget for a short time what had happened just previously. If you want the worst case scenario, then you should know that their presence can cause your entire memory to be wiped out."

The scene shifted into the next dream-a complete showing of yesterday's adventure.

However, at the end of the dream, it was as if the LuAstrien had succeeded in using the weapon to pulverise Anne. Even though this was not happening, Anne could feel the sensation in her body. Her whole body was stinging very painfully, and it felt as if her body was going the burst. Her brain, heart, and lungs actually stopped. Anne could do nothing. Even though she could actually not feel it, somehow she felt as if glass was stuck in every part of her body and that a very, very, *very* sharp knife had stabbed her. All these sensations that you wouldn't want to talk about happened all at once, maximizing the pain.

Anne woke up with a start. She had learned two things from that previous dream:

1.) That she never *ever* wanted to go through that again and

2.) Like Nohanga said about the memory, she must have done the same thing as Jane, but now she fully understood that the figures *had* mentioned Cartabania.

She heard a creak. Then, it sounded like something was moving in the distance.

Oh, no-not again. She had not liked what had happened the previous night, nor the dreams and sensations *to*night. But having to go through the events one more time, to her, was like torture.

71

But what happened next was different.

She heard another creak, then a crash from the distance. Then another creak. And another crash. Again and again! A lot more moving.

Every time it happened, it felt like the sounds were getting closer.

Closer.

Closer.

Closer.

So close that it felt as if it were happening right above Anne's head.

But then, the sound started travelling away from her.

Further.

Further.

Super-faint.

And it was gone. Just like that.

This was too strange for Anne. She had to get to the bottom of this!

She sat up, turned around her body, and got up.

"This is going to be a long night," Anne said to herself. *"Good night, sleep."*

She then realized that the only obvious way that this could have happened was because the sound was coming from the air duct system. But she was sure that this wasn't normal.

Before she knew it, she was trying to track the sound down by crawling through the system. However, what happened next was beyond ordinary.

She later on believed that all this happened because this is part of the system that actually is at the exterior of the craft-that the system is outside in space.

And then that's where Anne was-with no spacesuit on her.

Going to what happened at that point, it is this:

She entered some sort of area much wider than the parts of the system she was in before-it was like a very large room. She had no further need to crawl-in fact, crawling here would be impossible for most.

There was no gravity in this area. But it wasn't anything like back on Earth during training, or even when she was outside in space in her spacesuit. This felt like it was even *more* anti-gravity.

She had heard that true anti-gravity was when there was extremely close to no gravity.

But this was actually *no* gravity-a feeling you couldn't get unless you were in the same situation as Anne.

She floated around effortlessly, and swished her body around to change position and direction.

At points when moving her body, she did it as if she were swimming-right now, this was actually the easiest way to move around.

Though truthfully Anne wasn't a very good swimmer, at the current moment, it felt as second-nature as just walking-at an even easier position in fact.

At another point, she came up to the very top of the wide-open space and the metal surface at the top was like a ceiling, yet she could actually change her position so that she was actually walking on the ceiling-walking upside-down. It felt to her as if she was actually walking on the ground.

As she was walking, she later came to a surface that would really be a right wall. Without pausing for a second, she just walked onto it with ease, switching her position as she did this, but to her, it felt like walking onto an odd-shaped stair.

She played around with that a little bit until she fell into the exit of that part in the system.

Her body was in such a position that sliding through was really bruising her.

Plus the anti-gravity was starting to wear off, and then she was stuck. Up-side down.

Now that was how she would have to crawl. She crawled until she saw a pitch-black area.

Naturally, she was curious and continued on.

Before she knew it, she was falling down, going through some liquid freezing and hot at the same time.

It felt as if she were going through a waterfall of mucky water.

She fell into a dirty stream and swam to a "sidewalk" that reminded her of a subway tunnel's "sidewalk". There, she collapsed.

When she finally got back up on her feet, she thought that she saw a dragon-like figure flying away. She chased after her.

* * * * *

Anne couldn't catch up. She stopped to pant and take a breath.

It seemed as if the figure had flown up, and then soon, it was nowhere in sight.

All of a sudden the *Star Speeder*s axis shifted to its left side-up. Everything was rumbling. It felt as if the space craft had entered an Asteroid Belt! Which was weird, seeing that Anne had turned auto-pilot on, which could detect asteroids. So, why-

CRASH!-*KA*BAM!

A huge asteroid crashed through the area where she was! Anne was sucked into space!

Without a spacesuit.

PART 2

U gh! The feeling was horrible. It expressed freezing and boiling to death at the same time. Without a space suit, anyone would die instantly. So why wasn't Anne?

Anne held on tight to the railing of the *Star Speeder*. She travelled left to her pod. But how would she get in?

* * * * *

Later, she entered through the Emergency Entrance/Exit.

Anne headed over to her pod where Michael's controls currently were.

Someone (or something) had messed with the controls! And though it seemed very unlikely, Anne had a hunch that it was the dragon-figure.

Anne managed to put the space craft back on course.

She looked outside and saw that they were nearing some planet that strangely resembled the descriptions of Cartabania from *The End of Cartabania*.

There they would find the Ancient Scroll.

There they would find Michael.

They were there.

* * * * *

Switching To Log Format:

James here. This is the first time I'm using my Web Cam log for quite a while, and I'm liking it.

When Anne had piloted the *Speeder* near the planet, all of a sudden, the gravitational pull of Cartabania started to pull us in! At least Cartabania was all safe, and we didn't crash land.

Cartabania was like a desert planet. It was hot and dry like a desert, but it wasn't made up of sand. Instead, it was made up of the sort of iron that gives Mars its famous red look.

We would think: Could there be life here? Now, that I think about it, that was a pretty dumb thing to think.

So we started to look around-see if we could Michael.

After a couple of minutes, we found out that he was nowhere nearby.

We got back in our vessel to investigate using *it*.

Man-the whole planet was covered in caves. Apparently, Anne was also thinking like me-those caves might serve as prison cells. Michael could be in any of them.

Cave after cave, we searched in vain. Still no sign of Michael anywhere! But that's when I saw something drawn in the sand:

M C L T

It was four letters making absolutely no sense! But wait-M could stand for Michael. C could have something to do with "cell". L-it always reminds me of "location". And t-I don't know why, but I felt like it meant "top. So, it might've been saying "Michael Cell Location Top".

Michael must have put that there!

So the cell in which Michael is located, well, could have Cartabania's highest-or **top**-security!

MCLT. Got to

remember that!

I told the others' this.

"In my book, it said that the highest security cells were along the equator-26 in total. Every cell has a different letter engraved at the top," Anne told us. "Each for the hostages' last names. So Michael must be under "J"!"

That seemed like a good idea, so we decided to head along the equator.

But there was such a distance between these highest security cells. By the time we reached "C", an entire hour had passed!

I needed something to keep me busy, so I played a little bit of Pac-Man.

When I looked up next, we were at "I" now.

When I looked back down, in horror, I yelled, "CURSE BLINKY!"

You know, I guess I'm done with Pac-Man.

And in twenty minutes, we-had knocked into a wall. And we were more than 100 feet in the air.

The *Star Speeder's* engines failed and soon, we were plummeting down to the ground.

What seemed like a million years later, we got out, coughing up smoke. We were *definitely* going to have to replace those engines.

Panting, I took a look in front of us-there was a little opening in front of us.

Jane tried to walk through it, but it was like there was some invisible force field blocking her way.

Rohit thought that he could do something about it.

He got out a little toolbox and started building something.

I don't know what he built, except about 5 minutes later, he threw this weird glowing-orange box-thing into the opening.

KA-BOOM!

A big explosion. The whole huge wall started to collapse and we started to run away.

The wall caused a huge dust storm and I think I felt the smell of something burning.

Dustier than the dustiest dust storm on Mars.

More powerful than anything you could imagine.

Once the dust had cleared away, there were no remains of the wall left.

I looked at Rohit.

Note to self: do not underestimate Rohit.

We all started walking towards the "J" area.

A cave was there-completely unguarded.

Huh. This was going to be easy.

It wasn't really "Huh. This was going to be easy."

We had to dodge lasers coming up from the ground, jumping over opening trapdoors, running through openings between moving inwards spike-covered walls, and jumping with ease in the low gravity past bottomless pits (don't ask me how I knew they were bottomless. It's an experience I'm trying to forget.)

Finally, we entered the cave. It was empty.

All that hard work for nothing.

Then, I noticed something: a huge boulder next to a corner.

I put my hands in my space suit pocket-like compartments. There was a box of dynamite in one, and I had *no idea* how that got there.

But I wasn't complaining. I pulled a stick out and threw it towards the boulder.

KA-BOOM!

I bet Rohit's making a mental note not to underestimate *me*, now.

And standing right there was Michael.

Right then and there, Anne dropped to her knees right next to Michael.

From behind, I saw Rohit raise an eyebrow to Anne. I didn't know why he did that, but then, Anne said, "I never said what I promised about, now did I?"

We all shared our stories-like Anne's adventures at night. Michael told us that he didn't remember being captured or taken here, though somehow had an idea about the four letters.

MCLT

Now, that we'd found Michael, we had to get to Area #999.

And, what do you know? Before we knew it, we were there!

And there were no monsters or anything like that. Just a scroll that looked like it was from Ancient Rome or Egypt or some place of that sort floating around.

The Ancient Scroll.

Michael got out and took it back in.

We all gathered around in his pod. He opened the scroll. A flash of light blinded us. Then, it faded, and in the center of the papyrus was an elegant oval.

There was a photo of our next destination-the Taj Mahal.

* * * * *

Rohit here. I like this log. But it *was* strange when the Scroll turned out to be a photo of the Taj, in my old hometown of Agra in India. But here's the confusing part-Nohanga had said that the scroll was part of LuAstrien myths-probable eons before the Taj was built.

I needed to know more.

82

So I snatched the scroll from Michael exclaiming, "The Taj!"

Right as I said it, the scroll started shaking and a female voice said something in LuAstrien.

"What the-?" Jane said.

The same voice then said-in English, "English selected."

"The city of Agra has been of alien origin. All of those silly rumours about the Emperor Shah Jahan were merely a cover-up story for Earthlings. Ever since those blasted creatures humans call "dinosaurs" roamed the earth and when India was part of South America, we LuAstriens have been there. We built Agra along with most of India's cities, like Delhi and Mumbai. Then when India attached with Asia, we stayed hidden in forests and mountains, where most couldn't find us. But sometimes, we would go to the Taj Mahal, where our most guarded secret: sacred and religious to us, which if known to the outside world would be the end of our species, is hidden."

The scroll dangerously began to glow brighter and brighter.

"Shield your eyes!" I yelled.

And we all did.

When we opened our eyes, the scroll was gone.

But, hey-it's better than *us* getting destroyed!

And so, I guess I saved the day.

Well-one thing for sure.

We're going straight away to Earth.

Chapter 11
The Voice

Hi! This is Jane. James and Rohit make it sound less scary and exciting. It was truly amazing, but extremely scary.

Anyways, Michael began the auto-pilot heading to Earth immediately.

And just quickly, we heard a strangely familiar voice around us booming the five words: "Abort Mission Immediately. It's Suicide."

And echoed-again and again coming from no source.

But I think that he just *wanted* us to abort mission.

Why, you may ask.

Well, let's start here. We were just going through asteroids when all of a sudden-right where there were the most asteroids, they strangely started flying towards us at light speed.

"What the-?" Rohit started. We were looking through the huge glass windows at the top of the *Speeder*.

I'd never thought about it before, but it seems pretty dangerous. What if an asteroid crashes through the windows and we are sucked into space with no protection?

I talked to Rohit about this and asked if he might have an idea for protecting us. I mean, he was so into engineering and mechanics, so if there was anyone who could fix that issue, it would be him.

"Yeah-I've got an idea, all right," Rohit said.

"What?" I asked.

"Well, it's complicated to explain, but what we need is a method to get into Michael's pod."

"Talk Michael into lending it?" I offered.

"He probably won't cooperate with me."

"How about I do it, then?"

"He'd be suspicious. Besides, I have no wish to do something with *him*."

"Well, then who else can access his pod?"

"Anne can."

"So why not we ask her?"

"Something tells me she won't help either."

"But isn't she the only one with duplicate keys?"

"True. But still...."

"Why not you steal it?"

"I'm not that stealthy."

"Well, then what else can we do? We're doomed for sure, and I doubt we can auto-pilot away from those asteroids any longer."

"Well, there is one thing I can do."

"What?"

"We could ask someone stealthier than us."

"Who?"

"Only one other option."

"WHO?" I asked a little louder, though I think I knew who.

Together, we said, "James."

We found James snoring in his pod.

I was about to shake is shoulder to wake him up, but hesitated. You do NOT want to see James when you disturb his sleeping.

But I had to do it.

"Who-what?-but-oh…," James murmured. But then he came to senses and registered.

I started explaining why we woke him up a little anxiously. I had to exaggerate the details a little bit so he wouldn't think we woke him up for nothing.

"You mean-that's all?" he said calmly. "You just want me to steal it?"

"Uh-yeah," Rohit said.

James has one of those one-second-chuckles I find really annoying, "Well, okay. It's child's play, really. I remember one time when I was in kindergarten…."

"James?" Rohit interrupted.

"Yeah?"

"Just get going."

"Okay."

I thought it was going to be a long wait, but, surprisingly, James was back in just over a minute!

"Sorry I took so long," he apologized, which I found weird for two reasons-one being that he never apologizes. The other....

"Sorry?" I laughed. "James, you were awesome!"

"How did you do it?" Rohit inquired.

"Oh-uh-I walked up to Anne," James started. "And said-hey-I think Michael's calling you."

"Keep going."

"And she dashed away in, like, a second. And she left her pod open. When I was sure that she was nowhere near, I quickly crept inside and grabbed the keys from a drawer."

"I never knew that you were so-persuasive, James," I told him.

"Uh-huh. Well, now you know. But I got to go. Anne will be back any sec-"

"JAMES!" an angry voice yelled from across the corridor.

"Bye!" said James quickly.

"Thanks!" Rohit and I said.

We were so excited that we nearly trampled over each other while we ran over to Michael's pod and jumped inside.

Luckily, Michael was sleeping-lost in his dreams.

My first impression of the pod was, "Wow. Why don't I get a pod like this?"

From the outside, Michael's pod only looks a little bit bigger, approximately the same size, but up close there's a huge difference.

I could sort of make things out in the complete dark because of flashing light coming from the supercomputer, the keyboard buttons, and the controls.

They computer was built in to the front. With the keyboard and controls along it. There was a single comfy looking chair with controls on one armrest, so the design was like on a plane. It should have transformed into a bed with a king-sized mattress, except, for some reason, Michael was on the floor. Behind me, there was a box built-in to the wall with a glowing blue light, but nothing was in it. Then, I noticed some controls next to it, so that anything could show up there that you pick at will.

Everything in our pods is cozy while still high-tech.

It's really like you've never left home, just that it's more high-tech and awesome.

What I mean is is that our pods are nice and casual and just like a nice comfy, cozy apartment.

But with Michael's pod….

Everything was triple the size.

Everything had triple features.

Everything was triple awesome.

In other words, it was awesome.

Rohit started typing some binary language-lots of 1's, 0's, and some words in tags like <this> and </this>-on the computer with one hand, and was builder something-I guess I'll call it an "enhancer"-with the other hand. He told me to monitor those glass windows, and so I left immediately.

Right as I thought an asteroid was going to crash through, it disintegrated

Some others were coming. But all within 10 feet bounced away and those who managed to come any closer also disintegrated.

We were safe.

I ran off to Rohit to tell him it was working.

"What did you do?" I asked.

"Oh-it's a force shield," he replied.

"H-h-how does it work?"

"Well a magnetic force bounds things off and, well, our speed is so much that anything in its way will be pulverized."

"Do you think that this is what that voice was talking about?"

"I don't know. But one thing for sure. It has some super-natural power that can destroy someone light years away."

Chapter 12
The Invasion

It's Anne. Now that those asteroids are out of the way, I guess that we've almost made it there. I'd just seen Mars a couple minutes ago.

Anyways, the journey was pretty boring after the Kuiper Belt, so I'll get to the juicy part.

At the Asteroid Belt-no, that was pretty much the same as the Kuiper Belt....

Oh-this is strange:

Once we reached the moon, I saw-and I know this sounds strange-fire and lava, as if there was some active volcano there. Something that'll probably make you think, "What the-"

There was also a fleet of spaceships of all shapes and sizes, all looking as if they had alien origin, and I think I knew who that was. It was the LuAstriens. And they were ready to attack. I guessed the biggest one was the mother ship, or at least the mother ship for the attack.

They were going superfast – almost light-speed.

Almost.

But the *Speeder* could go faster than that. Even *more* than light-speed.

The *Star Speeder* is sweet!

"Michael," I said on my super computer. "Um...I think we should speed up to the *Speeder's* maximum."

"No," he told me. "That only works in plain ol' space. If we do that on a collision course heading towards Earth, we risk destroying the *Star Speeder*, and worse – creating an impact that could destroy the planet."

"We have no choice. Wait-if the *Star Speeder* is destroyed, will we die too? Wait-that was a stupid question. Anyways, we also can't risk the LuAstriens getting there first. And as we are speaking now, we're losing time."

"Well," He smiled. "I'll see what I can do. Hopefully, without getting burned up and disintegrating to no mass and end up compressed by gravity like a Neutron Star and end up a black hole."

I had thought he was joking. But as we entered maximum speed towards India, I thought we were going to be burned up.

Even at that speed, we barely beat the LuAstriens to Earth.

Well, hard to say since they were beginning their invasion in Beijing.

Once we landed right outside the Taj, we got out.

My first impression-HOT!

Well, I've never been to a place like India, but it feels as if you're going to boil to your doom. I checked my PDA for the weather:

Sunny and a 30 degrees *low*.

I hoped it was Fahrenheit, but, with my luck, it was Celsius.

I could see everyone else sweating and looking uncomfortable. Even Rohit, who's lived here in India for a lot of his life.

We started to walk toward the Taj (ignoring the extreme temperature).

Michael and Rohit were talking to each other, which I   thought was a good sign, but it turned out to be angry yelling. And I thought that could pretty much sabotage the operation.

So then, I got an idea.

I walked towards Jane and James.

A lot of complaints and asking what happened.

I told them to speak in a hushed tone.

"Okay," James said.

"What is it?" Jane asked.

"I've got an idea," I replied.

"What sort of idea?"

"Well, I'm guessing one that could make two problems we have as a crew solved.

"What?" James asked impatiently.

94

"And why aren't Michael and Rohit here? They're really crucial to the *Speeder*," Jane added.

"Well, about that," I said. "It'll make it a lot easier to conduct the operation and save Earth."

I could see that they were really losing their patience – especially James – so I decided not to keep them any longer.

One or two minutes later, Michael and Rohit, who were way ahead of us, came back to see what was taking so long.

And perfect timing: just as I finish explaining.

"Hey, guys?" I managed, sounding a little awkward. I wasn't sure how they'd take the news, so I didn't know how to word it for them.

"Yeah?" Michael asked.

"Well, we," I pointed at James, then Jane, and finally myself. "Were just discussing an idea that we have."

"Well, it better be able to wait," said Rohit (how typical of him these days). "We're losing time. Besides, it's only early September. You don't want to stay out long in the hot. Believe me, *I* know."

"Well, it's about that," I told them. "Well, actually, first of all, I just checked the PDA for the weather. I also got the date and time for New York. Halloween evening. Not early September"

"So that's what you had to tell us?"

"Rohit's right-and this is the only time I'll ever agree to what he says. We're losing time, so come on!" Michael said. And with that, they set off.

"No, Michael! Rohit!" I called. They turned around. "About that. Really! We're not coming with you."

"WHAT? No way are you leaving me with him," They said together, pointing at each other.

"I know, I know. But if we separate, we'll be able to get this done. We're losing time. We need to split up! There are only five of us and thousands of them. If we stay together in just one location, there'll be nothing we could do to stop them. Tell me this-how are you supposed to vanquish the enemy at the same time as discovering the Taj Mahal's secret while rocketing towards the deadline? Hmm? And either way, well, you two **_never_** agree on anything! That way, you'll sabotage the operation! There's already enough to fight-so we shouldn't fight among each other! You two have to learn to **_WORK TOGETHER_**," I put a lot of emphasis on those two words. I stopped to calm down and take a breath. Then I looked at Michael. "COOPERATION! I feel like I'm a first grade teacher telling my students this. And if you do it, Michael, there will be something in store."

"Oh-and Rohit," Jane added. "That goes for you as well."

I don't know what made it more convincing: my argument or that last part because they immediately agreed and before I knew it, they were off.

As I walked towards the *Star Speeder*, I turned back and saw Michael turned back, too.

96

That might've been the last time I'd ever see his face.

I walked into Michael's pod and pressed the "Switch to Pod 2" button.

Then I walked to my own pod and said "Crew: Ready for Take-Off?"

"Signal's clear," James said.

"Okay-we only have one chance for this in these skies," said Jane. "I am about to press the button to close the ground support. I will countdown until it is gone. You have to ready to take-off at that time. If we can't do it in the time-limit, a fire could start, the craft may explode, we'll be crushed by air-pressure, make an impact in the ground, blah, blah, blah, and who knows what-not?"

"Uh-huh," said James, who didn't seem that interested.

"Okay," said Jane. "T minus 10...."

I flipped down a switch.

"9, 8, 7, 6...."

More switches.

"5, 4...."

I typed something on my keyboards and punched down a lever.

"3, 2...."

I pulled down a pulley.

"1!"

I pressed the Launch button and we successfully made lift-off.

We all cheered.

Our plan was to head to Beijing to see if we could stop the LuAstriens before it would be too late.

Actually, we were about to go to all of the major cities in our path: Beijing, Tokyo, Moscow, Baghdad, Rome, Paris, Madrid, London, maybe even towards Toronto, Vancouver, San Francisco and New York!

We skipped Delhi and Mumbai since it seemed unlikely the LuAstriens would have invaded their own home territory.

Wow. We made it to Beijing in no time! But it was too late. The entire area was on fire and there were no sign of any buildings. I could only hope that the citizens were safe. Ashes. Everything burned. All covered with dirt and stuff like you see in some movies.

As we pondered this, we flew around China. No sign of any life. Buildings were burned down everywhere. This was the work of a bomb even worse than nuclear!

We dashed away to Tokyo. Nuclear power-plants were blown up, buildings burned to ashes, and still no sign of life. And it was like that all around Japan.

I felt horrible: our job was to protect human lives, and we've probably just killed over a billion people.

"We're landing," I said.

"No!" said Jane. "The pollution and smoke will kill us!"

"We have no choice. We have failed already. If three more lives are lost today, what does that mean to the aliens? Over a billion people have died in just ten minutes. How are we supposed to protect the entire population of the world? What is three lives compared to all that? What are three lives compared to over 7 Billion lives?"

No answer.

I take that as a, "Nothing. Fine, let's go outside."

We landed and got into our spacesuits. That could protect us from all this.

We explored for a while. We didn't find anything that would help us in anyway. Our reason-*my reason*-for coming down here is for something to explain what was going on.

After a minute or so, we decided to split up. I started heading east, James went west, and Jane explored North, South, and pretty much everywhere else.

I walked and walked with no luck when all of a sudden, I stumbled. It was then that I found out that I was standing on a part of Mt. Fuji. It had been blown up. But I had no time to react to my discovery-I was on tallest, steepest and slipperiest part.

I tried to come down, but it was so slippery, that I fell!

99

Luckily, I grabbed a support just in time, but it was about to fall out!

I started up right as it fell out. Whenever my feet touched a support, it would fall out. It was a miracle that I got to the top.

And as I got up, my way back fell off! There was nothing I could do! Well, actually, there was one thing, but it was like suicide! Still, I had no choice.

I jumped.

And, yeah, I was screaming some heroic battle cry like, "AHHHHHHHHHHHHHHHHH!"

And it was the Oh-My-Gosh-I'm-About-To-Die-Screaming-And-Panicking Type.

I don't know how, but I lived.

I fell onto another slippery chunk of the mountain and soon, I was sliding to my doom!

But, no! I slid up into the air and fell onto another chunk! And it kept on going like this for a while.

It was sort of like a roller-coaster, except its *way* scarier in real life.

I fell into this tunnel, and slid inside this huge chunk.

I fell and made quite an impact.

I groaned and got up.

But I couldn't believe my eyes. There-underground (well, at least before my impact), was a bomb. It looked like it had some alien origin.

And next to it was a horrifying sight-the skeleton of the alien that put it there. The LuAstriens were enslaving their own kind to place bombs and then, since there would be no longer need for the attack group, the enslaved LuAstriens dies doing it.

I felt angry-really angry, and then, I know this sounds weird, but the power in my rage seemed to explode the chunk!

BAM!

A million pieces flew off in all directions.

I ran off yelling, "Jane! James!"

I knocked into Jane-literally. As we both got up, I told Jane about my findings, "What did you find?"

"Oh, uh-the Bullet Train derailed by the aliens and this," Jane held up a glass fragment. "I think this is important."

"Yeah," I said in a hurry. "We'll examine it onboard. But right now, we have to find James. Unfortunately, he's pretty fast. He must be way ahead of us."

"You're forgetting that he comes back in 30 seconds if he doesn't spot anything that seems interesting. That's when we set up a time. He'll be back soon."

"This is way too long, though. He must be in trouble!"

"They what are you waiting for? Let's go!"

We had the run of our lives.

And if it were a recipe, it would look like this:

Run Of a Lifetime

Yield: 10 Seconds

Materials:

1. **Two** Young Adults.

2. **At Least 1** Destroyed Major High-Tech City By Aliens From A Worse Than Nuclear Bomb.

Procedure:

1. Jump over this!

2. Duck under that!

3. Dodge over here!

4. Fall under there!

5. Repeat Approximately A Hundred Times.

But then, Jane spotted a suspicious-looking ring of fire.

Coming closer, we saw James! And he was trapped inside!

We didn't have any water on us. What could we do? Then, I spotted a water tank. I sure hoped this worked....

I used a bullet to open it.

Water splashed everywhere, and the huge flames died down a little. Must be some LuAstrien fire.

Without thinking, we ran through, which, thinking back on, is pretty dumb.

Then, I saw the LuAstriens. A whole army of them!

They shot their pistols at me, but I easily side-stepped. I saw James and Jane fighting them.

A LuAstrien shot James' gun out of his hand. And Jane needed loads of help. I reached to pull out my own gun, but it wasn't there.

I looked around desperately trying to find it. And then I saw it. On top of the water tank.

I jumped over and ducked under bullets. Then I grabbed my gun.

It was a furious fight. James, left with no weapon, tackled some down, but there were still dozens left. The LuAstriens were too fast for Jane, and she couldn't get anyone of them. I managed to get several of them, but it wasn't much. We were losing.

But then, when I thought back to my rage exploding that chunk of Mt. Fuji, I got an idea. I just hoped it would work.

I let my rage take over me until I wanted to scream, but not much happened.

But then, I got it! It was *power* that did the trick – not rage.

I started shooting and my shots became more powerful and powerful. I shot down 6 of them with one shot! Then, my power started to let go and it seemed to go down to the ground. Then, BOOM!

The LuAstriens fell towards the ground.

Together, we raced back to the *Star Speeder*.

Chapter 13
The Taj Mahal's Secret

Hey. Michael here. So Rohit and I were walking towards the Taj Mahal.

"We have to take off our shoes!" he said.

"Not under these circumstances!" I countered.

We ran into the Taj Mahal.

I was thinking that we would need an expert at Indian stuff.

So, I hated to admit I needed his help, but I would have to.

I stared towards Rohit.

"What?" Rohit asked. "Why're you looking at me like that?"

"You have the best chance at finding something out," I told him.

"Why me?"

"You lived your childhood in India."

"Uhh-okay," It did not really seem like he wanted to say "Okay" to me, though. "Follow me."

I ran off to wherever Rohit was heading.

I know that he was just trying to get around the conversation.

Now, the Taj Mahal really is beautiful if you want my opinion, but, unfortunately, right now, I had no time. Maybe I'd come back another time. That is, if we succeed and the Earth isn't destroyed, conquered, or all of the above.

I mean-this is a lot to handle. The stake of the entire world is in our hands. A lot of people think this is really cool with all that action and adventure and all, but, believe me, if you were in the same situation as me, you wouldn't find it all that cool.

Finally, Rohit stopped next to this wall. There was some symbol on the wall-it was in Devnagari, the way of writing of Sanskrit, the old language of India.

"Do you know what this says?" he asked me.

"Um...no," I told him.

"Om," he said it like saying the letter O, then M's sound, the M continuing for a second or two. Join those and you've got Om!

"*Om*," he said. "Probably the most powerful word for Hindus."

"Okay, but how's that important right now?"

"I'm not sure."

We continued walking for a while when

BAM!

We were standing right on top of a trapdoor, and now, we were falling to our doom!

SSSSSsssssssss.

A hissing sound: not very reassuring.

Rohit and I fell on top of-grass.

Then all of a sudden, something emerged from the grass-a snake! And not only any snake: a King Cobra!

Rohit and I ran around, trying to avoid it. Unfortunately, he had many minions, and right as we got the perfect angle to shoot the Cobra, the unthinkable happened.

We ran out of bullets.

We knew that we were doomed. We closed our eyes for our last silent prayers.

The hissing got louder and louder, and I knew the Cobra was getting closer and closer.

I braced myself, but then, the hissing stopped.

I slowly opened my eyes and saw that the Cobra was disintegrating.

It's too ugly to describe, but I can tell you this: when I looked at my feet, I saw there was a toxic puddle.

I don't how it got there, but I was just glad we were safe.

We managed to climb up with great difficulty.

We had to avoid spiders, falling pieces, you name it.

When we got to the top, we collapsed on top of the floor.

After a couple of minutes, Rohit got up, and I did too.

We were still in the Taj Mahal, but it seemed like a different area. Maybe it was a hidden chamber, which I think it could be. But that wasn't what was strange.

What was strange was on the floor:

It was a spaceship.

* * * * *

Well not really a spaceship, more like a little enclosed chamber than looked like a London telephone booth.

But it was *not* a telephone booth.

Rohit and I went inside it. It was a little crammed with both of us in it.

However, there was no phone there. Instead, there was an eye scanner like one you might see in a superhero or super-spy movie.

When it looked at it, it scanned my eyes, and it looked like an alien technology.

It made a strange beeping sound.

Then, it shot straight up into the air.

* * * * *

We were going so fast that it felt like my face was peeling off. Seeing the speed, most people probably didn't see us.

The alien "telephone booth" kept going higher and higher until we were up in space.

Now-don't ask me *how* it happened but it flew at light speed and crash-landed on the moon. But not just any part of the moon-the dark side.

Luckily, we weren't hurt. We tumbled out (literally), and fell (accidentally) into an enclosed crater. Well, not really a crater. It was sort of a volcano, except most of it was underground. I mean-only 2 or 3 feet were about the ground.

Inside, it looked a bit like a volcano on Earth from the outside, with cracks with lava everywhere.

But what was interesting, which I bet you won't see anywhere else, is an elevator sticking out of a pond of magma.

No-not like the type you'll see in a mall: more like those old wooden box-shaped types with ropes.

Rohit and I crammed ourselves inside, careful not to fall. We still weren't talking that much.

But the second we got on, it started moving-not up or down-but it moved from side to side: left to right; forward and backward.

I knew we were in for a wild ride.

Finally, after a couple of minutes, we went through this small gap. It didn't see that important at first.

But then, it felt like we were entering a whole new place. We were easily 500 feet above the ground, and *this* part was way deeper than the first part of the volcano. No wonder that was only 15 feet.

I was looking out at the ocean of magma, thinking that we were really lucky that we didn't drop down here, instead of that other part when the unthinkable happened.

It broke.

I knew we were toast.

But that's when I saw a couple of meters worth of rock at a corner which we could land on.

It would be a huge risk, but, hey! We'd die anyways.

"ROHIT!" I yelled over the sound we caused from falling through the air. "EXTEND YOUR HANDS AND LEGS LIKE YOU'RE GLIDING! MOVE TOWARDS THE LAND!"

We glided towards the rock-land.

At first, it looked like we could do it, but we were about to hurtle into the magma ocean.

We completely lost it.

We tried flapping our arms and legs to see if we could turn into birds, and I know how that sounds, but you'd probably do the same thing if you were in our situation. No such luck.

We closed our eyes and braced ourselves for the second time that half-hour, but then, another miracle happened.

We landed safely.

Rohit and I sighed with relief.

But that didn't last long.

I saw a huge blob of magma that seemed to become bigger and bigger.

But then I realized that it wasn't getting bigger and bigger-it seemed to be coming closer to us. When it got really close and saw what it really was, I was horrified.

It was a huge fire-breathing dragon made entirely of magma and lava, or coated with it. I managed to make out Igneous Rock underneath, though it looked melted, but I wasn't about to put my hand on it to make sure, so I won't ramble on and confuse you. It also had Stegosaurus-type scales going down its back.

Rohit and I were frozen with fear. But then it roared fire, and we came to our senses.

We saw small rock-platforms along the sides if we could scale it. There were oozing lava cracks everywhere, and some of the rocks were crumbling

111

down. It would be a longshot, and if we fell, there would be nothing we could do this time.

But we would have to try.

Rohit and I basically trampled each other trying to climb up.

We started climbing.

We managed to avoid the lava cracks.

We jumped from platform to platform.

We would have to be precise to jump before the platform crumbled off.

But we managed to do it.

In fact, we were really good at it.

Before we knew it, we were almost at the top.

Sometimes, the dragon would fly up and try to grab or burn us.

It had huge, scary, bat-like wings.

In fact, at first, to keep me from being frozen with fear again, I tried to imagine him as Batman about to save us.

But, when he tried to grab me, well, let's just say my strategy stopped working. Plus, it was easily 100 times the size of Batman.

Luckily, apparently it would need to absorb magma to fly, and when all of his lava and magma would fall down, it would glide down and absorb more, which gave us lots of time to proceed.

As we would get higher and higher, it would become harder for the dragon to catch us in time.

Soon, we had little ways to go.

Only several more jumps to go….

5…Nothing should happen.

4…Don't crumble too fast.

3…Almost there.

2…Please.

1! Only 1 more jump!

Rohit was already at the top.

He was waiting for me.

It was this huge platform stable enough not to crumble.

If I could successfully jump up there, we could crawl through a small opening and escape.

And so I started my jump,

It crumbled exactly then.

This had happened before, and I was successful each time.

But I didn't jump high enough.

"Noooooooooooooooo!!!!!!!!!!" I exclaimed.

And I fell to my doom.

Chapter 14
New York Battle

Anne: We managed to escape blasts from the ground, but unfortunately, they had friends in the air with a whole lot of firepower.

But it was all too hard.

So then, I tried something foolish *and* dangerous.

I made the *Speeder*'s gravity increase.

And then, at the brink of when we were about to be crushed; at the brink of when the alien air craft were going to collide with us, I got rid of all gravity, quickly moved ourselves higher into the air.

The aliens weren't fast enough and knocked into each *other*. I saw an explosion below us.

Then, an entire other fleet started descending from the moon.

They looked exactly the same, like something a kid might draw as a UFO: a base and a glass dome for an alien to see through.

But one of these was way larger-the size of an entire country!

(Well, I admit it, not a **huge** country).

Luckily, they didn't see us.

They stopped their descent right in front of us.

They still didn't see us.

But we saw them. (How can you miss the mother ship?)

We started following them.

They went on to the next major city in Asia.

While the rest of the fleet, including the mother ship, stayed level, one descended for an invasion.

We shot it down just in time.

It seemed like the fleet didn't notice it, and they stayed put for a minute.

Then we followed them towards the next major city, and shot down another invading U.F.O.

It seemed as if they still didn't notice.

This time, they didn't stop.

We kept following them to the next major city.

The same thing happened.

We kept following them, and the same thing happened every time.

And they went in this weird zigzag pattern.

They went to Europe for places like Madrid, Paris, and London (they almost knocked off the Eiffel Tower and the Big Ben!)

Then, they backed off to Africa for a couple of cities, like Cairo. (They still didn't notice us, but there were a couple of close-calls).

They kept going South, and just when I though they would start invading the penguins of Antarctica, then went up North to South America.

There, we went to places like Rio and Brasilia.

Up in North America, they tried New Mexico City. The alien mother ship still wasn't doing anything.

We skipped mainland US and went over Hawaii. Luckily, they didn't invade there. (It was where I would have my victory celebration).

Then, in Canada, there were a bunch of cities that the invaded, like Toronto, Vancouver, Montreal and Calgary.

We went back down west for the Western United States. We would go from coast to coast. We stopped at places like San Francisco, Los Angles and Chicago. The mother ship *still* wasn't doing anything.

Soon, it was only the mother ship left in the fleet, but it still didn't notice anything.

It came to a screeching halt, if there was such thing in mid-air.

We were above Manhattan, New York City when it turned around.

Then they noticed us, and a battle had begun.
* * * * *

First, from the bottom of the base, it sucked up the entire area of the Chrysler Building, and then opened up a gap for a fleet of thousands of UFOs, each about one story square.

I didn't want to know about *that* technology.

James went totally berserk, and it took Jane quite some time to calm him down.

Then, they both went to the sides of the *Speeder*, where there was a thing that looked like it could fire pirate cannonballs, but it used giant bullets and lasers instead.

I could shoot from where I was.

And I guess we were pretty good. We were shooting down UFOs in no time.

But the Mother Ship was firing as well, and would suck up more and more buildings for more and more enemy craft.

It was very overwhelming. The chances of us succeeding were probably very low.

We swerved from side to side, avoiding fire. We also had to avoid buildings, and we succeeded with that (mostly).

Buildings would crumble down and explode.

It was an intense battle over New York.

We were firing and avoiding simultaneously.

And that became very hard.

Luckily I remembered about Rohit's shield feature. The one he used to save us from the asteroids of the Kuiper Belt. After turning it on, it became a lot easier. But not easy enough.

117

It was still very overwhelming.

We flew down there and aside buildings.

We flew out there from inside buildings.

Dozens of fleets were chasings us. We made a 360^0 while flying past way up in the clouds. It was getting hard to avoid them and we ended up flying straight through a large window in an office building.

Glass flew this direction and that direction. Some even fell through James' pod window causing him to whine, "But I just got this fixed!"

We made an 180^0, and then turned back upright.

We flew by sideways past buildings and then went along the shore of the Atlantic.

The *Speeder* had been trying to escape the mother ship.

Then, strangely, the mother ship disappeared towards the Statue of Liberty, and I didn't have a good feeling about that.

It had just recently swallowed up the Empire State Building, and so things were still looking pretty bad. It was looking very good for us. It was millions of UFOs with way more powerful ammo than us against one powerful but relatively weak *Star Speeder*. Oh- and did I mention that it wasn't looking very good for us?

Then, in a split second, I got an idea.

The co-leader would be on the Mother Ship, right? And the Leader of the LuAstriens, well, I would just have to hope Michael and Rohit were okay. So by taking down the co-leader, this battle would be done once and for all.

And so we chased after him.

And the entire fleet chased after *us.*

We would swoosh down here and race past there to avoid constant fire.

The mother ship was trying to lose us.

Were we going to let that happen?

NO!

Oh-and did I mention the constant fire?

So we kept following and blasting him, no matter the great difficulty.

And considering all of the UFOs chasing after us, boy it was hard.

It was an intense speed chase.

We were almost there.

Almost there….

BAM!

Greeeeeooooooooooooooohhhh.

A UFO shot an engine right off!

We were almost at the island, but we were still well above water.

"We can do it," I tried encouraging everyone.

But I first needed to encourage myself.

Oh-and did I mention one of our engines flew off?

We were slowing down and descending at a drastic speed.

How would we ever get back across?

I watched in horror as the Statue of Liberty was sucked up into the Mother Ship, and pieces were falling into the water. Lady Liberty might not *ever* be rebuilt.

We started back towards mainland. Seeing all the fire coming from all directions, it would be suicide anyways.

But we were actually making good time.

I lost some concentration and wondered why there were little pedestrians in weird costumes, and why they weren't running around in fright.

Then I remembered: it was Halloween.

Those were kids trick-or-treating, and they probably thought this was some cool fireworks show they were watching, and they didn't know that the world was at stake.

But I spent too long pondering on all this.

Over the Astronomical Voyagers Academy, the alien mother ship shot down the other engine.

And with the *Star Speeder* on fire, we hurtled down towards the ground.

* * * * *

With a big explosion, we tumbled out. It was a big miracle we were still alive.

But we had failed. The entire world would be destroyed, all because of me. I led this operation. I thought about Rohit up in space. I thought about Michael. All the UFOs had stopped, and were aiming down at the city. Down at us. I would never see him again. A tear went down my face.

Weooooooooooooooooooooooow!

Then, another miracle happened.

Hundreds of giant aircraft, only a little smaller than the *Star Speeder* soared up into the air from the Academy and started firing at the UFO's.

It was an intense battle happening above our heads.

They were facing the same challenges as us, but however, even though there were still more LuAstriens, our side began overwhelming *them*.

Hundreds of explosions were happening at the same time.

Soon, the mother ship was down, and so were all the other UFOs.

We had won!

Or had we?

Amazingly, the LuAstrien co-leader fell from the sky.

He was still alive from the explosions and the fall.

This would be an easy one to take down now.

He headed into an apartment complex, and we followed him.

We chased him up an apartment. He had no intention to fire back. He knocked on a door.

"You knew," I started. "You knew that we were following you."

"Of course!" he said in a deep, gritty voice. "That's what I told everyone during the first of my fleet's invasions! That was the wait. I told my plan."

I was about to keep talking and soon, fight back, when the door opened. We were out of sight of the two kids that opened the door.

Apparently, they were about to leave themselves.

"Trick or treat," The co-leader said.

I tried not to laugh, despite the situation. But it's hard to resist. He did *not* sound like a kid wanting candy.

"Hey!" said the taller kid. "Nice costume."

"Yeah. Where should I put the candy? Really nice costume," added the shorter kid.

And those were their last words.

I don't really want to describe it; it was really disturbing.

But I'll say this: it had to do with gnashing teeth, blood, and screaming. Oh-and cannibalism.

With the last two kills, the LuAstrien expanded in size.

He was growing and growing at great speed.

The building collapsed.

Soon, he was at tall as the Empire State Building. Well, as tall as it *was*.

Everyone focused all their fire on him.

But he was bullet proof. He started chasing us.

And then, we ran.

* * * * *

Let me just say, it was a fierce chase on everyone's part.

We ran through the city.

He kept picking up buildings and throwing at us.

Luckily, we were too fast, and the buildings exploded. I felt sorry for everyone in there.

Then, we reached a dead end.

From here, it was water. And he was gaining on us.

We tried swimming away.

Hey, you would be out of your right mind, too!

Somehow, when he reached the water, he started evaporating.

And he was stuck.

Soon, there was nothing left of him.

We came up on shore, and all of New York City cheered.

We had one this New York Battle.

Now, I could only hope everything was going fine with Rohit and Michael....

Chapter 15
Volcano Battle

Michael:

Then a hand grabbed me.

I looked up at the smiling face of Rohit.

He pulled me up.

"Thanks," I said.

Looks like we weren't against each other anymore.

But we had work to do.

We couldn't just cower in fear up here.

That dragon was the LuAstrien Leader.

For the world's sake, maybe the universe's sake, we would have to fight it.

Then, the dragon picked up Rohit and moved him towards a plank shaped platform, down low.

I would have to save him!

But I would have to act fast before the dragon would breathe fire, Rohit would inhale too much smoke, or both.

Then, I saw a tunnel system on the platform.

I moved quickly through, desperately looking for Rohit on a plank-shaped platform. After some time, I found something reflecting blue on the ground. I picked it up.

It was a sword.

It was shaped like something knights would use.

The sword reflected blue off its gleaming, sharp blade. I was careful not to touch it.

As soon as I lifted the sword, I felt more powerful, like I could do anything.

I quickly and silently named it *"The Blue Crystal Blade"*.

I soon realized that I was now at a dead end, and I saw this last opening over here should be where Rohit is.

I got out walking onto the seemingly plank shaped platform.

But it wasn't plank-shaped, and I almost fell off! But my reflexes had become faster because of the sword.

As I said, I felt more powerful; more intelligent; more brave.

I saw that Rohit was actually at a platform just a little further and a little lower than me.

But it was too big a gap for a jump. But I would have to try.

No. I couldn't.

But I would have to help Rohit.

It's too risky.

You have to.

Don't do it.

These are the things that crossed my mind.

It was like there were two tiny voices in my head, like you see in cartoons. One seems evil and selfish. And one is good hearted and kind.

The sword has some other-worldly power (which seems pretty likely) that made me jump.

As if in slow-motion, I jumped down towards Rohit.

I was about to fall.

I put my hands out in front of me.

And I grabbed and pulled myself up.

Then I went in front of Rohit and lifted my sword to strike.

* * * * *

I know how I'm making this sound so quick, but my reflexes made me this quick.

Right as I was about to stab at the monster, it breathed fire at me.

Somehow, my sword reflected the fire back at the monster, shooting blue sparks everywhere.

I stabbed experimentally.

It swerved its body to avoid it.

And we got each other's fighting styles.

We started a fast-paced battle.

I kept reflecting fire back at it, but it had no effect.

It would shoot fire, and it was getting harder to side step.

I moved my sword through the thick air around me.

No effect.

It was like it had some sort of force shield around it.

Then it had its largest breath of fire.

I couldn't reflect it this time. It hit it with my sword's hilt only, and then, the fire turned to ice.

I slashed with it.

The LuAstrien Leader slowly froze like into an ice sculpture and shattered.

We had won.

* * * * *

Now I won`t take too long to tell you how we escaped, so I`ll just fast-forward to when we were returning to Earth.

Rohit managed to build something the size of my pod to take us back.

And we were having a nice, luxurious journey.

But then, when we were descending down through the atmosphere, it caught on fire.

We didn't have anything to protect us, and when a part fell off, we were rotating rapidly and tossed down into the air.

I felt like I was burning as I fell down towards Earth with no protection, no landing gear.

It was just a huge drop down.

And now, I *really* fell to my doom.

Epilogue

November 1ˢᵗ, 2011 3:00 P.M. EST: Michael woke up in a hospital bed.

He slowly moved his head around to observe his surroundings. He ached with pain throughout his whole body.

To his right, he saw Rohit, also in a hospital bed. Apparently, he had just woken up. A digital clock on the wall said it was 3 P.M.

Rohit had an oxygen mask, probably from the smoke he had inhaled from the dragon. Michael didn`t have one, but he too looked like a mummy: bandaged head to toe.

On his left, he saw a window overlooking a beach with several palm trees.

From a door on the right, three people walked in.

It was Anne, Jane, and James.

"So you're awake," said Anne, smiling above him.

"How long was I out?" Michael managed.

"Oh, almost a day."

"How do you know?"

"We found you and Rohit falling from the sky in our vacation spot at about midnight. Well, Jane and I did, anyways. James was sleeping."

"Wait a sec. Your vacation spot? Where am I?"

"A hospital in Hawaii."

"What?"

"I'll explain later. The doctor said you'll be out of the hospital soon. Oh-and is this important to you?"

Anne held out *The Blue Crystal Blade*.

After exchanging stories for a while, Michael insisted on getting a team name. After a couple of suggestions, Michael said, "How about 'The Voyagers'?"

Everyone liked the idea.

Michael then said, "Well, then. I guess that's it. The Voyagers Unite."

To Be Continued In:
Star Voyagers:
Book 2:
The Humanoids Attack

A Cool New Website: Coming Soon!

Check Out An Animated Comic Web Show By Ishaan Sahai:
Ninja Adventures Beyond
ninjaadventures.webs.com
Also By Ishaan Sahai:
Space Explorers

Bonus Features:
What Ishaan Says

A Look at the Next Book

The Making of STAR VOYAGERS

What Ishaan Says

Dear Whoever-Is-Holding-This-Book-Right-Now,

Hey! You're probably here now because you've finished reading *Star Voyagers Book 1: The Voyagers Unite*. Well, that is unless you were skipping to the back to find out what happens at the end. You didn't do that, right?

Well anyways, I hope you enjoyed the book. If you want to find out what happens next to Michael, Anne, Jane, Rohit and James, the next book will be called *The Humanoids Attack*. Things will only get more interesting from there.

I'm also the author of *Space Explorers* published with KidPub Press.

Following are some Bonus Features!

Find out what will happen in the next book!

Find out more about the origin of Star Voyagers!

Bye.

Sincerely,

Ishaan Sahai.

A Look at the Next Book

Michael Jefferson and the rest of his crew: Anne, Jane, Rohit and James own the amazing *Star Speeder*.

The previous year, they had saved the Earth from aliens: the LuAstrien species.

But their adventure is far from over....

The crew, known as the *Voyagers* have been called on by the Academy.

Strange things have been happening. Strange sightings. Many have disappeared. But these strange sightings are by humans-or at least they look like the.

And just when they think they can rest easy, an astronaut of the *Voyagers*, James, gets kidnapped himself!

Now it is up to *Michael* and the rest of the Voyagers to find James and save the world again from the so-called **HUMANOIDS.**

The Making of Star Voyagers

The five-book series follows the so called *Voyagers* who own an elite *Star Speeder*. They repeatedly are saving the world from aliens.

But how did the series ever come together?

Ishaan Sahai had started writing his first book at age 8 in the 3rd grade. It was called *Space Explorers* and was meant to be something he was writing just for fun, but his parents wanted it to be published. At age 9-and a couple days away from age 10-it finally became published in the 4th Grade: January 2010.

Ishaan now wanted to write even more. So, he came up with Star Voyagers and began writing the first book that very February. He finished writing in his 6th grade at age 10 in December 2011.

The first book is called *The Voyagers Unite* in which the adventure begins. Michael and crew earn an amazing *Star Speeder* and, before they know it, are out in space. Their mission: nothing. It was just a joy ride. But before they knew it, they were saving the Earth from aliens called the LuAstriens.

The adventure continues in *The Humanoids Attack.*

Then will follow a Book 3 and a Book 4.

The adventure will be concluded in Book 5.

By: Ishaan Sahai

Made in the USA
Charleston, SC
22 January 2012